AIRPLANE BOYS IN THE BLACK WOODS

Airplane Boys #7

By **Edith Janice Craine**

(Originally published 1932)

Presented by ithink books

ithinkbooks@gmail.com

The Airplane Boys accidentally bump into a new mystery which is only solved after many pages of excitement in this seventh book of air adventures.

TABLE OF CONTENTS

Chapter X
An Invitation

Chapter XI
Revenge

Chapter XII
The Fight in the Passage

CHAPTER I
A RECEPTION COMMITTEE

"Holy Clover, that fellow would make his fortune in a dairy, all right," exclaimed Bob Caldwell glancing over the side of the plane the Flying Buddies had borrowed while the "Lark," their own splendid machine was undergoing much needed repairs at the shop of the British hangar in Belize.

"His fortune, how do you make that out?" Jim Austin demanded. "I'll bite, let's have the answer."

"He'd do the biting—that one tooth ought to be great to make holes in Swiss cheese!"

"If I didn't need both hands you would get a wallop that would leave you only one tooth, then you could start competition," Austin answered. "Well," he added as the plane came to a stop, "this sure looks as if you will find enough different kinds of vegetation, old Horticulturer, may your tribe increase."

"Sure does," replied Bob with an eager light in his eyes as they went from one great tree or vine to another. "Wonder who dropped that one-toother down in this place." The one-toother was a tall, emaciated, dark-skinned individual whose age, judging by the wrinkles on his body and face, was in the neighborhood of two hundred. His lips were thick, eyes sunken so deep in his head that they looked like burnt holes in a blanket, his huge mouth was wide open and from the upper jaw was the lone tooth. His only garment was an irregular bit of tiger skin suspended from a narrow woven grass belt which looked as if it might once have been decorated with a long fringe but only a few of the strands of its ancient grandeur remained. It was impossible to tell, either by his features or color if the man was a native Indian or one of white blood who had been tanned and re-tanned through the long years spent in the tropical climate. He stood perfectly still facing the plane but the boys were not sure if he was staring at them or not.

"Suppose he's alive?" Jim whispered.

"He looks as if he'd been there as long as the trees," said Bob, then he raised his voice. "You're looking hearty," he called. At that the queer creature of the forest gave a slight shudder which went from the top of his bald head to the soles of his bare feet, one bony arm was raised a few inches from the side of his body, and almost instantly he disappeared. "Exit, the gentlemen from where!"

"Where in the name of Mark Antony did he go?" exclaimed Austin in amazement.

"Reckon we came, he saw, and fled," supplemented Bob. "Let's have a look about. Perhaps we'll have the pleasure of seeing him again, but we don't want to get too far from the plane, Old Timer, and we'd better watch our step. We are two little lads far, far from the home corrals and my guess is that that lad wasn't impressed with our looks."

"Too bad," lamented Bob.

"Yes, reckon you wanted to study that vegetable," Jim grinned.

"He didn't look like any variety of life I've ever run across."

The Sky Buddies climbed out of the cock-pit carefully surveying their surroundings and listening intently for a sound of the vanished ancient, but if he had never been near the spot it could not have been more quiet; not even the buzz of an insect disturbed the silence. From the air the boys had soared above a dense forest and it was only by chance that Caldwell had noticed the small clear space and suggested that they land and see what it was like. The clearing was less than an acre of hard soil with a ridge of sharp rocks which protruded like saw-teeth diagonally across. It looked as if sharp-edged slabs of stone had been dropped when the soil was less packed; or it might, hundreds of years before, been the top-most edge of a wall so arranged as an added protection against animals or tribes that might attempt to scale it. As the ages had passed accumulated vegetation, falling or shifting rocks, and sands blown from distant miles have filled in the space leaving only this trace of what it once was.

Beyond the clear spot, which was highest in the middle, sloping somewhat like a dome, was the forest. Great trees whose ancient trunks were hundred of years old, grew straight and high. The majority of them, as far as the Buddies could see, had almost no low branches, but their massive limbs started more than half way up the boles, and each one overlapped with his neighbor so thick that the intense sun could not penetrate the foliage. Beneath were smaller growths, many with long tangled roots twisted in grotesque shapes as they clung like giant arms to the rocks and disappeared in the soil. Huge vines with stems as large as a good-sized sapling, clung tenaciously as they climbed upward, and many of them were in bloom which gave the place the look of a particularly beautiful bower.

A few feet from where the boys were standing was a basin, into which a spring of clear water trickled from the crevice of a rock. That too had the appearance of great age for the opening through which the water had found its way, was worn in a smooth, deep groove. The basin itself was about three feet across in the widest place, and nearly as deep where the spring fell into it. From the lower edge it ran off in a tiny stream, winding about until it disappeared into the forest.

"If we hadn't seen that oldest inhabitant I'd believe that ours are the first human feet to hit this place. Say, it's kind of spooky, isn't it!" Bob exclaimed softly.

"It does look as if it has been waiting for a million years," Jim admitted. His eyes were searching the dome-like surface of the place upon which they were standing.

"Wonder where the old boy took himself. He might be Enoch. Looks old enough. Perhaps he just dropped down from heaven to have a look at the world; maybe wanted to see if it's changed much."

"Go on, he'd wear wings instead of a piece of tiger skin," Jim answered. "What do you expect to learn around here, Buddy? You never can get into the forest, not far, anyway, and you ought to be able to see the same sort of growths where it's less isolated."

"Surely, expect I could, but me hearty, the Elephant's Child has nothing on me for curiosity, and now I'm here—"

"All right, Old Timer, I'm with you to any reasonable extent, but you remember how said Child got his nose pulled. Careful where you put yours," Jim remarked.

"I'll keep him in mind," Bob chuckled.

"Have a look at this," Jim's hand waved to designate the clearing. "Suppose it could be the top of some temple that's been buried by earthquakes?"

"Might," Bob agreed thoughtfully and examined the place more closely, but they kept close to the machine. "Reckon we'd better watch closely; that chap may come back with some more angels."

"He might. Lucky we took Bradshaw's helicopter instead of one of the other machines."

"Yes, even at that I'd rather have the 'Lark'."

"Why not wait until she is fixed up then come back in her?" Jim suggested. There was something awe-inspiring about the whole scene and he felt that they would be safer with their own plane, which had numerous extra instruments, greater speed, and was infinitely more easy to pilot than the Canadian Mounty's machine.

"Aw Buddy, we want to get home sometime! I say, we started out, expecting to be gone not more than a couple of weeks and look how long we've been hanging around down here. I'd give a tooth right now to fork a real bronc and have a grand gallop across the ranches."

"Same here," Jim nodded with a little sigh.

"But since we are here I'd like to see more of what grows in this climate. We have to wait for the 'Lark,' the message tube is safe in the hands of Don Haurea instead of in your pocket—"

"Or Arthur Gordon's," supplemented Jim.

"Wow. I say, I bet a jack-straw against the White House that he was congratulating himself that we didn't take it back from him when he was laid out so nicely—"

"I'd give a pair of colts to have seen his face when he opened the empty one. Silver pants, but that was a streak of luck—"

"I'll say it was. That was a mistake as was a mistake," Bob chuckled. "Gee, when I saw you let him take it away from you without so much as a yelp I might have known it was flukey. We couldn't put up a fight, all tied around like a pair of hot dogs, but you didn't even squirm. And you never knew that you'd sent it by the mail pilot from La Paz—"

"Didn't discover it until just before Gordon's gang flew over the 'Lark' and dropped the big boy on our wings. Some stunt that was, you have to hand it to him—"

"Yep. I'm going to get the lariats then have a look around; also a drink of water. That spring looks good enough to be the fountain of life. Bet the old lad who was here must have filled up on it to renew his youth."

"You nut. Going around by the woods?"

"Right the first time. I won't go out of sight though. Maybe you'd better stay here. My massive brain informs me that if some fellow should come along and round up that plane we'd be in a fix."

"And how. There are miles of those woods."

"Then some." Being cowboys of no mean standing, the Flying Buddies just naturally unhooked their ropes from their saddle horns when they changed from a horse to a plane, and on more than one occasion that habit of their lives had helped them through several mighty serious and tight spots. Now

Caldwell got the two lariats, which had been transferred as a matter of course from the "Lark" to the good-natured Canadian's helicopter when they started on this observation trip. Bob hoped he might discover, among the wild tropical growths, some fruits, roots or herbs which could be raised advantageously on his mother's own ranch, the Cross-Bar in Texas. He was intensely interested in flying, thoroughly appreciated the joys and practicality of air travel for either long or short distances, but his love for the land and what might be done with the great acreage he would some day own, was uppermost in his thoughts. The horticultural and chemical department of Don Haurea's immense laboratory was the one from which he derived the greatest satisfaction; while electricity and mechanical sciences fascinated Austin.

"Taking them both?" Jim asked.

"No, thought you might like to have yours handy."

"Thanks, Old Timer. Maybe you'll see how Enoch got away."

"He had no wings so must have dug-in or crawled." Bob strode off briskly toward the edge of the forest, leaving Jim, the rope hanging loosely in his hand, to see that nothing happened to the plane. Austin watched the younger boy stop at the lovely spring, scoop some of the clear water up in his hand, and take a good drink. "Great stuff," he called. "Feel as if I'd knocked off ten years."

"Go on," Jim grinned. "Don't drink any more. I do not know how to take care of infants."

At that, Bob shied a stone that struck the ground within an inch of his step-brother's foot, then proceeded. He reached the rim of the thick woods, where Jim saw him pause, then start slowly around, scrutinizing everything that grew. Keeping one eye on the lad, whose white suit made him easy to follow, Austin glanced around at the ground and began to wonder what it had been and what it was. Since his acquaintance with Don Haurea he had seen and been inside many marvelous underground caves, temples, ancient hiding-houses, homes of the once famous race of the Yncas, as well as their vast laboratories. He knew that the lost empire had extended no further north than Quito, hundreds of miles south of them, but he knew also that at the time of the Spanish conquest of the Americas, this northern portion of South America had been inhabited by intelligent Indians whose origin none could trace. They too had built amazing temples, and it occurred to the boy that five hundred years ago, when the remnant of the conquered tribe had gotten together, some of them may have been mobilized from localities far from their original homes. It was not straining credulity to reason that some of the temples of the northern tribes might have been utilized to advantage, and certainly this dome-like clearing of rock, with its gurgling spring, might be over one of them, and the water might be forced through the stones so that the moisture would assure the underground community, if there was one, of dense growths which would be an added protection against invasion of their domains.

Jim remembered that the first time they had landed on the high plateau, known to Peruvians as Amy Ran Rocks, they had found an ancient Indian woman apparently in possession of the place. At that time she had recognized the green emerald rings given the Flying Buddies by Yncicea Haurea and had told them to 'go in peace' but today, the ancient who had stood like a man struck dumb in amazement, had made no such identification. Thinking it all over carefully, Jim decided that the Amy Ran guardian was probably apprised of the boys' coming, while this man, if he watched an ancient fastness, had heard nothing of the Flying Buddies.

"Then, again," Jim grinned. "This may all be perfectly natural land, formed so through the ages, and the Indian a lad who lives in the forest as far from the whites as he can get. Our dropping down on him was a surprise, and the minute he got his wind, he beat it. Just the same, his exit was mighty sudden. He was standing near the water, then he just wasn't. I didn't see him run an inch or drop, but he surely did fade out pronto."

That fact stuck in the boy's mind, and now Bob was some distance from his starting point, so Austin moved to the front of the helicopter lest he lose sight of the youngster. There was an uncanniness about the place, and Jim wished that his step-brother would hurry with his investigations, but he appreciated the fact that Bob was thoroughly interested in what he was doing, and that it would be unfair to urge his step-brother to shorten his investigations. They could not possibly linger in the country many days and this opportunity seemed like an especially good one which should be made the most of, while it was possible.

Suddenly, from the east, Austin noticed a thick white cloud moving swiftly toward the coast, and forgetting Caldwell for the moment, he studied it in puzzled wonder. It certainly was not vapor of any kind, it was too substantial looking, and another thing he observed was that it did not move with the wind, which was from the south, although the breeze did affect its direction somewhat. As it drew closer, he noticed that it was considerably deeper than when he first picked it out against the sky, also from its midst tiny particles, almost like snow, seemed to hesitate and fall.

"What in heck?" Jim had his field glasses slung in a case from his shoulder, and now he hastily took them out and in a moment was examining the strange phenomena. "Well, what do you know about that!" he ejaculated.

Magnified by the glasses, the boy saw countless small, white butterflies, fluttering and poising in the sunlight. There were myriads of the tiny insects flying toward him, and as they came, hundreds of their number dropped out and tumbled toward the ground as if too exhausted to continue their journey. As the boy watched in astonishment he had no idea of what it was, then suddenly he remembered reading that every year the butterflies, their life work completed, start in a tremendous migration, drifting southeasterly along the sea coast until they finally reach the sea, where they drop exhausted into the water and die by the millions. He knew that science is unable to explain the strange instinct which prompts them to choose death sometimes thousands of miles from their breeding ground, and only a few weeks before he had read an article by someone who had seen this great funeral cortege when it hovered near a steamer. As the boy recalled, this migration usually took place in the autumn, but he decided that probably in different localities the time of year differed.

"Gee, they must be mighty tired," he exclaimed pityingly, "and I'll bet they are leaving a thick white track beneath them." They were getting so close now that he no longer needed the glass to see what they did. The outer edges of the "cloud" were thin, as if leaders or scouting parties were racing in advance, but from the main body so many were falling that they must have appeared like a strange sort of storm. Several minutes more he watched, then he remembered his step-brother, and glanced in the direction where he had seen Bob a bit earlier, but no white-suited boy stood out against the dark background of the dense foliage he had been examining, and Jim's heart jumped into his mouth.

"I say—" He moved in the direction Caldwell had been going, then he stopped with a gasp, the shout died on his lips and for the moment Jim was too paralyzed to make a move.

About half way between the plane and the rim of the woods he saw three tall natives, their bodies naked except for the tiger-skin and the grass belt such as the ancient had worn; their heads adorned with a high dress of peacock feathers whose many colors shone brilliantly in the sunshine, in one hand each held a long spear with a glistening point, while the other held a number of small, deadly-looking darts. One of the men had an arm raised, his body was bent slightly toward the woods, and from his extended hand shot the javeral, cutting sharply like a hissing knife through the air, and to Jim's horror, it was flying faster than the eye could travel, toward young Caldwell's unsuspecting back.

CHAPTER II
KIDNAPPED

As Bob Caldwell pursued his botanistic observations along the edge of the dense forest, his mind was filled with keen regret that he could not spend several weeks in the neighborhood with plenty of reference books to aid him in recognizing the numerous varieties of vegetation which surrounded him, and he also regretted the fact that they had found the old Indian, or whatever he was, in the neighborhood because of course that meant that the spot was not so isolated as it appeared and in all likelihood there were others living close by. But for the appearance and disappearance of the mysterious old man the Flying Buddies would not have felt the need of such caution and he could have been confident that it was safe to penetrate a little way into this paradise of tropical growths and perhaps find something they could take back to Texas. It was disappointing, but at the same time he had to admit that it was doubtless better that they had discovered him immediately; better than thinking they were secure then running into a hostile tribe without warning.

Since they had come to South America the Buddies had encountered so many dangers in wild, out of the way sections that it had developed their bumps of caution to a high degree. To be sure the authorities had quietly ascertained that Arthur Gordon was still laid up with a broken leg at the home of the doctor who had taken him in charge after the accident in the snowy fastness of the Andes, and Ynilea, the Laboratory man at the Don's had said that the Big Boss, frightened at the repeated disasters which had befallen many of his men and undertakings, had taken himself out of the country, but the Sky Buddies were convinced that this chap, whoever he was, had made up his mind to fathom the secrets and secure possession of the vast wealth. While the loss of a few lives might make him get away, to save his own skin, he would probably recuperate his weakness, reorganize his band and start in again at the first opportunity.

"The Big Boss, I reckon would get back to the United States, or to his own hangout, wherever it is, cure himself of his scare, then begin all over again. Getting possession of unlimited wealth, he'll figure, isn't to be passed up, and this time he'll cook up some schemes that may work better than the others." Bob grinned to himself at the idea, then through his brain flashed the memory of the wonderful laboratories with their numberless workers and scientific advantages. "Then again, maybe they won't. I'm betting my dimes on the Don."

With that comforting assurance, Caldwell turned his attention to his job, moving slowly and occasionally glancing across to where his step-brother waited patiently beside the plane. He thought that Jim was mighty decent to hang around doing guard duty when he would probably have liked to do some studying himself, and resolved to cut his observations as short as possible. With that in mind he snipped leaves, tiny branches, bits of root, and made rough notes to which he could refer later when there was more time. Nearly two hours had been consumed and the younger boy had made half the circuit when he reached a section where there were almost no large trees, although those which grew on both sides were so heavy with branches and foliage that the arch above was as thick as a roof. In the space there seemed to be more fallen trees and rocks than elsewhere. Besides, there was a good deal of young growths, slender saplings and brush, also rather a heavy hanging, like a great curtain of vines suspended from the limbs above. The appearance of this semi-clearing made Bob suddenly remember the way they had once gone to the Laboratory with Ynilea. That day, the party had started from Cuzco by automobile, left the main thoroughfare, traversed an unmarked route over rocks and foot hills, finally leaving the machine and making their way through a well-concealed natural hallway until at last they came out on a ledge from which they were taken in a strange airplane the rest of the journey.

"Great Christoper's ghost, wonder if this is another of those hidden ways," he exclaimed excitedly, and forgetting for the moment the need to be cautious, he stepped on to a broken stump in among the protecting curtain. But, before he could advance another inch, his quick ear caught a sharp whistling sound which he thought must have come from Jim's lips, but before he could turn about, something dark cut in under his arm, hit the nearest sapling and drove like the blade of a stiletto clean through its heart. The young tree quivered from the impact and in an instant tiny beads of sap oozed from the wound.

"Whew—" Bob waited a moment, too startled to think, then he managed to turn about, and his eyes nearly popped out of his head. In the first place, it seemed to be snowing for the air was filled with fluttering white things which seemed to be struggling to go on, and although they looked like butterflies, the boy was sure he must be mistaken for he had never seen nor heard of anything like it. Through the queer storm he could see Jim crouched near the helicopter, the looped lariat hanging from one hand and his mouth open as if he had been about to yell a warning which had frozen on his lips. Quickly Caldwell's eyes swept to where Jim's were staring and instantly he understood from whence the murderous dart had been driven. He saw the three Indians, two of them facing him while the third had his gaze fixed on Austin. One of the men held a second dart in his hand and was slowly raising it above his head prepared to send it with deadlier aim than the first.

Then, as if some supernatural power had intervened, the fluttering white things dropped thickly into the space, completely filling it with their bedraggled bodies and helpless beating wings. As Bob stood a bit back in the protection of the swinging vines it was like observing the strange spectacle through a window. None of the insects landed within a couple of feet of him, but beyond the air was like a swirling blanket which effectively cut him off from sight of the Indians plainly determined to kill him. Anxiously the boy wondered about Jim, for he could no longer see anything but the butterflies, and through his mind raced half a dozen plans.

Bob thought of running out to his step-brother, but hesitated about doing that lest Austin endeavor to reach him among the vines. Thinking it over, in a moment the lad decided that his Buddy's best bet was to remain near the machine. Probably, safely hidden from the view of the Indians he could climb into the cock-pit and prepare to take immediate flight, then Bob wondered if the mass of insects would interfere with a take off.

With thousands of them tumbling about the plane their tiny bodies might clog the engine, propeller, and lifting wings, besides making it practically impossible for the pilot to tell in which direction to start.

Recalling the position of the plane when they landed, Bob realized that if the butterflies had done no damage the helicopter could mount without difficulty in the limited space, keep climbing until it was above the danger zone and they would be safe. With this fact in mind, he determined to get to the machine without further loss of time. It would take only a few minutes to be a safe distance from the Indians who could do nothing more until the air cleared. Then he recalled that the natives were doubtless familiar with the locality, they were the best woodsmen in the world, and the three might, even now, be making their way to him. The idea wasn't a cheerful one, and Bob turned his eyes in the direction he thought he had left his Buddy, then stepped forth. He had hardly reached the edge of the waving vines when he heard the unmistakable, although muffled roar of an engine and guessed that Austin was all set to go, but he was surprised that the sound seemed to come from further south than he had calculated. This fact made him pause to make sure, then, at his left he heard a noise of someone running. It might be one of the Indians so he drew back quickly.

"Buddy, I say, Old Timer, where are you?" It was Jim, not one of the natives, and Caldwell sighed with relief.

"Here," he answered.

"Good." Jim leaped beside him grinning broadly.

"Wow."

"I wasted a lot of time running around the edge but I was afraid of missing you," Austin panted.

"I heard the engine going—"

"No you didn't, not ours," Jim answered.

"But come along and we'll get it going."

"Must be another plane around here."

"Reckon there is and it may be as well if they do not see us," the older boy responded. "Great guns, these butterflies are life savers all right."

"Then some. It's like a nightmare."

"Put your hand over your mouth so you don't swallow a carload." Bob followed directions, and the Buddies bent forward prepared to start, but by that time the approaching plane was making a thunderous noise for it was above the clearing, then its motor was silenced.

"They are coming down, Jim. Think we'd better stay here?" Bob suggested. "We can hide out further in the forest."

"Reckon our best bet is to get to the machine," Jim answered, but then the plane came down so close to them that they could see its huge bulk only a few feet away. To get by it without being seen would mean some maneuvering and good luck aplenty. The boys scowled, but Austin motioned to proceed, so they stepped forth, bending low and praying that the newcomers would not look about them immediately.

"These blasted bugs," one of them swore roundly.

"They gummed the works," added another. There were half a dozen passengers in the plane who climbed out of the cockpit on the further side, then one of them called:

"We're right where we want to be."

"Good work," came a more cheerful response.

"Good pilot you mean," spoke up one.

"Pilot nothing, up in that buggy blanket you didn't know your prop from your tail; whether you were going or coming, upside down or right. Rotten piece of piloting gunning into a flock like that."

"I did not go gunning into them. The things came along so thick I couldn't get out of them. They got all over the plane and plastered everything, look at it, even my goggles are covered with them. I got you down without a smashup, didn't I? You can thank me that you're not hash—"

"Well, I'm not thanking you," the other retorted, then added with an oath, "and if you had busted the plane, I'd a pumped you full of lead, see. You can thank me that you aren't a sieve this minute." During this disquieting dialogue the boys had made little progress, then suddenly a voice shouted.

"I say, who else are you expecting?"

"Nobody, you know very well."

"There's a plane here—"

"A plane?"

"Yeh. One of those whirligig ones." At that announcement the boys stopped in their tracks.

"Let's go back," Bob whispered, tugging at Jim's coat.

"This is a hard crowd," Jim admitted. They started to retrace their steps but by the time they reached the fallen logs, the air was almost clear, the live insects had struggled on, while only a few who could go no further, fluttered to the ground, which was white with their fallen mates. Instinctively Bob's eyes sought the spot from which the dart had been thrown at him, but it was empty; there wasn't a native in sight, young or old.

"They are gone," he gasped in astonishment.

"Look who's here!" The Flying Buddies had been discovered by one of the gang, and a tall ugly looking customer who carried a gun in his hand, turned quickly. "Our welcome guests."

"What are you doing here?" the tall fellow snarled.

"Dropped down very much as you did, I reckon," answered Jim.

"Bugs drive you out of the sky?" This was probably the pilot who had just been driven out himself.

"Like blazes. That motor hasn't been running lately. If the bugs forced you down, what you doing over here? Come on, speak out, and reach for the sky, while the reaching is good," came the sharp command.

"Aw, be yourself," Bob retorted angrily. "I'm not reaching to anything for a goof like you—"

"Aint you—" The gun pointed threateningly, then one of the men interposed sharply.

"Put it down, Mills." It was the smallest man in the crowd who gave the order and he strode forward. "What you fellows doing here?"

"Came up to study the vegetation," Bob replied firmly.

"Yeh. Well now, that's nice. Where do you hail from?" Jim's foot sought his step-brother's, but Caldwell did not feel the pressure.

"Texas," he answered, and immediately he wished he hadn't been quite so specific.

"Couple of flying cowboys. Well, you'll never know how glad we are to find you here," the man sneered.

"Oh, don't mention it," Caldwell answered with a cheerful grin, but both of the boys were wondering what new mischief was afoot.

"I won't mention it outside of our little circle of friends here," the fellow promised. "Nobody'll ever be able to say we run across you in these parts. It'll be our little secret." He turned to his companions. "Remember that, men, this happy meeting aint to be whispered to any naughty inquirer."

"Sure. Now, give us the dope."

"It's the—as I said before, THE kids we need in our business, see! Be sure you see, and hear."

"Gee, aint we got luck!"

"The Don's own little pets."

"Waitin' fer us. Aint that thoughtful now."

"Hope we didn't detain—"

"Shut up," snapped the little man, then turned to Bob. "What you doing here?"

"I just told you, studying the vegetation."

"Yeh, well that stuff don't go with us. These here Honduras is full of vegetables, see, you don't have to come way up here."

"We were flying and saw this clearing so we came down. Whether the 'stuff' goes with you or not, it's the truth. My brother is interested in things that grow out of the ground and we looked for a place cwhere—" Austin started to explain, but was cut short.

"You mean you was lookin' fer this place."

"No we were not. Have a look at my specimen book if you want to see for yourself what we are doing." Bob proffered the book which was bulky with the things he had gathered and the small man glanced at it indifferently.

"That's a stall. Now, you got something in your possession we want; that tube of reports. Fork 'em over pronto."

"We haven't a tube of any kind," Jim answered.

"No? Search 'em boys." This was done roughly and thoroughly but not a tube did they find and they scowled when they finally had to admit defeat.

"Go through the plane," the tall man proposed. At this the pilot and two others raced to the machine, and in a moment it was being subjected to an overhauling that promised to leave it a wreck.

"Can't find the thing," the pilot shouted.

"No?" The little man drew his gun. "Now, you know what we mean. Where is that tube?" He pressed the weapon to Jim's belt and his rat-like eyes blazed with anger. "Where is it?"

"We did have a tube," Bob answered.

"I know you did and you still have."

"You are just as much mistaken as if you'd burned your shirt. We had a report tube we were taking home to Jim's father, but you're all wet—too late—"

"What do you mean?"

"It has already been stolen," Bob told him.

"Stolen! Who the—" The men were crowding around now and every face was ugly.

"By a friend of yours, I reckon," Jim drawled.

"Friend, hey—" The man whirled on the members of his gang.

"Turn that gat, you fool—"

"Who took it?" the little man thundered.

"Gordon, fellow named Arthur Gordon," answered Bob.

"Gordon, who the blazes is Gordon?" demanded one of the gang.

"I know him," the tall man answered.

"So do I, blast his hide. When did he steal it?"

"Day before yesterday. We were coming north; he passed over us in a big plane, dropped on the wings and drove us off the course. We landed up in the snow, had a fall, and he robbed us—"

"Yeh. Say, tell that to the marines. Gordon wasn't risking his neck by dropping on you out of another plane," the tall man objected.

"Then let you get away. You got to make up a better story than that, bo, see!"

"I do not need to. Gordon hurt himself and is laid up with a broken leg—"

"If he snitched the tube, then you got it back—"

"We didn't get a chance," Bob declared.

"Say, we'll fix 'em so they tell better stories. Tie 'em up boy with them lariats and do a good job. They got out of some tight holes, but the fellow that lets 'em get away this time gets plugged, see."

CHAPTER III

THE HORRIBLE CAVERN

There was no use resisting the gang for the six promptly jumped to the task of securing the Flying Buddies with their own lariats, and every man of them saw to it that there was no possible chance of them getting out of the bonds.

"Now, let's take these nice rings—"

"Let those rings alone." It was the tall man and he spoke so sharply that the would-be thief paused.

"Say, how do you get that way?"

"I'm telling you, let them alone, don't touch 'em."

"Aw, what's eatin' you—"

"Listen, if any man jack of you touches those rings, I'm through, see, I quit right now—"

"Yeh, well, we aint grievin' none."

"What you got on your mind? What's the matter with the rings?"

"You weren't with the Big Boss as long as I was, see, and maybe you never heard his orders to steer clear of green rings, 'specially emerald ones. Lord amighty, his brother shot a guy one night fer taking them two rings."

"Shot him!"

Through the Flying Buddies' minds flashed the recollection of the night when the De Castro plane had been driven through a raging storm only to be brought down by members of the Big Boss' gang, including young Gordon. That was the time when the four were bound on a ledge and a fellow who wore a tight green costume and close fitting mask, had appeared, called the men to task for what they had done, and later been frightened away from the spot by the ingenious Ynilea.

"Yes. He said his brother's orders were not to touch the rings, and don't I know once in Chicago a guy brought one in, said he'd picked it up in a hock shop, and the Big Boss kicked it through the window into the lake, that's what he done."

"Yeh. Well, what do you reckon's the matter with them rings?"

"Sounds like a lot of stewed tripe to me," declared the chap who was determined to possess himself of the jewels.

"Maybe it does," retorted Mills, "But I'm tellin' you to leave 'em be. I asked one of the lieuts en' he told me that a long time ago, when there wasn't no white folks in the U. S. er down in these parts either, there were rich Indians."

"Go on, Indians aint rich."

"Shut up, some of 'em were and are. Well, the whites came along, and saw them all dressed up in gold feathers, the women wearing ropes of diamonds and pearls big as eggs. It made 'em sore so much wealth goin' ter waste, so they shot a mess of 'em and took the stuff. Only a few was left and they were good and sore, so they dug hiding places, deep ones in these here mountains, and they took a lot of the best green stones they could find and made 'em into rings—nice ones that a fella would like to want fer himself en maybe fer his girl. Then, when the rings was all ready they took them to their temple on top of one of the peaks, and they prayed fer weeks and weeks, then they cussed them rings up one side and down the other. Cussed everybody who got a look at one, cussed all his family, and put some extra cussin' on the white guy who carried one, even fer a minute. Then they prayed some more to make it stronger, and they cooked up a lot of meat on the temple and the smoke all went straight into the sky, meanin' that the cussin' had took, see! Then they passed them rings around here and there so they'd bob up fer a long time and raise Sam Hill with any white man that got hold of one," he said impressively.

"Cussed 'em, eh." The chap straightened, and despite their predicament, the Flying Buddies had difficulty to keep from roaring with laughter at the strange recital. "Aw, I say, these fellows has been wearin' 'em!"

"Sure, en aint they outta luck?" That was evident to the gangster, who resolutely turned his face from temptation and such glaring misfortune.

"Say, you guys know the way outta here 'cept by plane?" Mills demanded suddenly.

"No we do not," Jim replied emphatically. He recognized the questioner as one of the men who had been on the ledge the night they were captured with the De Castros.

"Quit wastin' time on them. Come on in this place en we'll see where it's leading," proposed the pilot. "We aint none of us hankerin' to hang around here."

"No we aint," responded Lang. "You take that whirlgig plane en fly her where she won't be spotted—"

"I aint flying no plane that can be spotted side every other one between here en Medicine Hat. En what's more, I aint leavin' my machine while I go off some place else, see. How'd I get back, you goop—"

"That'll do—"

"Sure it will, but when I leave, it's in my own cock-pit, see."

"Yeh, en when he goes, I'm goin' long," spoke up a red-headed fellow stepping beside the pilot, his fist dug menacingly in his pocket.

"Oh, keep your shirts on," snapped the leader. "I fergot you couldn't get back. Can you cover the machine up so if any one flies over she wouldn't stick out like a sore thumb?"

"Sure," the pilot agreed readily, then he and his pal strode off to the helicopter. "Get the boys to chop us some vines," he called.

Paying no further attention to their captives, the men set to work with a will and soon the two planes were so effectively covered with foliage that only a very close observer in the air would have suspected for a moment that they were not clumps of underbrush which had sprung out of the rocky crevices. Cautiously Mills and his red-headed pal examined the work and finally pronounced it finished.

"And we can get it off quick if we're needin' to leave in a hurry," Mills announced with satisfaction.

"That's good," Lang nodded.

"What you going to do with those bozos," the red head demanded.

"Take 'em along," came the short answer. "Untie their feet so they can walk." Two men set to the job and in a few minutes the Flying Buddies were loose enough to stand but their arms were securely fastened and each rope had a length left dangling so that their captors could keep a firm grip on them.

"Now, step lively—" came the order.

"You got to give us a minute so the blood will circulate in our legs," Bob protested. "They are like pin cushions."

"Kick 'em around and they'll be good enough," Lang answered. "Move on, we're going."

With a helpless glance at each other the boys kicked and bent their knees to relieve the discomfort, and in a moment they were being marched behind the red headed fellow into the opening where Bob had stood when the butterfly "storm" started such a series of misfortunes. Caldwell had been in the place before and he knew that the soil was softer than out in the open, so now, on a pretense of limbering his stiffened limbs, he took very short steps, bringing each foot down hard so that his shoes left a heavy imprint. He was thankful that he had not worn soft soled shoes that morning and that his heels left a larger mark than those made by the feet of members of the gang.

Jim observed this activity on the part of his step-brother, and added to the clue in the trail by kicking bits of brush and sand with his toes. If by any possible bit of luck pilots from the British town found where the pair had been spending the morning almost anyone could be trusted to discover in which direction they had been taken. He managed to glance over his shoulders to see if the men coming behind him had thought of the possibility, but they were stepping quickly, for Red-head was leading at a lively pace.

"Go on, you don't need to stop to kick all day. Your legs are good enough," Lang snapped suddenly.

"Yeh, you're holdin' up traffic."

"They feel better now," Jim grinned cheerfully, but both boys continued to make a track whenever possible.

The way they were following was undoubtedly some path used by either natives or woodsmen traversing the dense forest, and the further they went into it, the more convinced the boys were that they were proceeding along a secret trail built by the ingenious natives. Overhead the leaves and vines grew in a thick mass and soon the route began to grow darker and darker, but Red-head kept going, feeling his way with his feet until they were making very little progress.

"Come on, get the lights out," Mills growled.

"Sure, nobody can see a light in here now," Red added. He did not produce a flash himself, but two of the men in the rear did, sending the rays on the floor of the trail. On they went at a quicker pace.

At times the forest cave lead them down steep declivities where it was evident to the Flying Buddies that the enclosure was made by hand, not nature, although she had helped. Another time they were walking forward on a woven floor and through the loosely secured vines they caught glimpses of sparkling water which pounded against the rocks that confined it and sent a spray so high that the place was spongy and wet. Later they were close to the surface of the stream and the boys guessed its bed was an underground passage. At this point the route turned sharply to the left and presently the flooring ended; they began to ascend a gradual incline which they judged was a circuitous path through some rugged section of the country.

It seemed to Jim that they must have been going for hours. His feet were beginning to tire and his calves felt as if every muscle was strained. He wondered about the Indians they had seen before the bandits came down in their plane and marveled more and more that nothing was done to impede progress. By that time they began to climb, and now the foliage was more dense, the air grew hot and stifling, as if the enclosure had not seen the light of day in many generations. Thinking it over the boy concluded that this route was rarely used and it certainly was not so well constructed as the hidden trail from Cuzco which he had traversed months before. In the first place, that was both light and the foul air driven out, then he remembered that it was cared for by the men in the great Amy Ran Laboratories from which it was constantly purified.

Austin tried hard to keep his mind clear and reasoned that perhaps Lang had in some way discovered the bare spot in the vast Andean forest, and may have investigated it, or he may have learned of it while working for the Big Boss. Then, overcome with greed, he had organized this handful of men to explore with him, calculating that the haul they would make would give each greater wealth if they were not forced to divide what they found with the whole organization. It struck the boy as odd that so many of the gang members had started out on their own, and each must have been thoroughly convinced that untold wealth lay at the end of this "rainbow" and they were eager to risk their lives in pushing their own discoveries to the limit. It was disquieting to realize that such a number of small groups were viciously determined to fathom the Don's secrets and reap the benefits of the riches which rumor carried like wild fire among the outlaws.

Following the wiry Red, Caldwell marveled at the strength of the little man who leaped briskly ahead as energetically as when they first entered the opening. Through his mind ran a series of plans for their escape but with arms bound, ropes held by grimly determined gangsters who doubtless had guns ready to fire at the first false move, the situation appeared utterly hopeless. He, too, was beginning to feel fatigue, his feet seemed weighted with lead, and his head and lungs ached from the foul air. Occasionally he glanced back at Jim, who kept as close as possible, but they spoke no word as they went on and on. At last the journey was telling on all of the men, for their panting breaths were coming in painful sobs. Even Red faltered; twice he slipped and almost fell flat, but he managed to recover himself.

"Better let someone else take the lead," Lang proposed.

"Better stay where you are," Red snapped angrily. Nothing more was said, then the boys began to wonder if any of the gang would drop out from exhaustion, but as far as they could tell, none had. Then one of the lights grew dim, and Red cursed.

"Change your battery." This was done, and soon they were going on swiftly, but there was a steep climb ahead. With difficulty it was finally negotiated, but it took nearly half an hour. At last they were all on the top. The place looked as if it crossed, or followed a high ledge, the wall which was moss grown formed one side, while the other was slanting, like a shed roof. Again they passed over a stream, but it was a mighty dangerous undertaking, for great holes yawned beneath them, and Red managed to make it by hanging on to the vines above him.

"We can't catch hold," Jim protested.

"Go on." Mills gave them a boost, and after a struggle they were on the other side. Then the way descended again, and suddenly the air seemed to clear.

"Whew, this is better," Mills gasped, with relief, and they all paused a moment to inhale deeply.

"There's daylight," Red shouted a few minutes later, and with a bellow of joy, he sprang forward. His shout changed quickly to the snarl of terror, and a shriek of abject fear. The Buddies saw his feet slip from under him on the log he was crossing. His arms shot up in a frantic effort to catch hold of something, then his body twisted and dropped from sight, leaving a great hole in the rotten tree. An agonized wail split the air, then all was silent.

"What's the matter," gasped Lang fearfully.

"Quit shovin', the thing's rotten as hell," Mills snarled and he threw his weight against the men who were pressing forward. "Get more light."

Two more flashes were produced, illuminating the spot. It appeared as if half of the great log which was suspended from great boulders, had given way. The lights revealed a deep, narrow cavern, they could hear water gurgling as if it formed a passage for a small spring or stream, and after fumbling with the light, Mills finally was able to locate the huddled body of the red-headed man. Silently, and shivering, the group stood for several minutes.

"I'm going back," Mills announced positively.

"Yes, come on." As if they were one man they turned about.

"Don't be quitters," Lang urged. "This air is better than back there and we must be almost out."

"Yeh, well, I'm going back." The ropes which bound the Buddies were not forgotten, and in a minute they were retracing their steps, this time with more lights than when they came forward. Although Lang argued that they were giving up when they had almost won, no one paid the slightest attention to him. They seemed to forget their earlier discomfort and went swiftly until they reached the last stream.

Again they stopped suddenly. The woven bridge, or flooring had broken at the edge and was dangling forty feet away. Mute with horror, the men stared paralyzed at the calamity.

"There's no way to get over," a gangster sobbed.

"Maybe we can chop our way through the roof," one suggested. He caught the side of the natural wall and hauled himself up, but when his ax struck the roof it rang against solid stone. Besides the stuff upon which the fellow was braced, gave way, and he slid back with a howl of fear.

"That log wasn't all rotten," Lang declared. "Come on back and at least we can cut some of the vines, make it stronger and get out that way."

"Yeh, en get pitched down with Red—"

"If you can think of anything better, suppose you get busy," Lang snapped at him.

"All right, I'm comin."

"Let them kids do the leadin' this time," Mills proposed, and without further ado the Flying Buddies were turned about and forced to head the march back.

"Give us a chance with our arms," Jim urged.

"Nothing doing, you go ahead. If you slip we'll haul you back."

They had to be content with this uncertain promise and in a moment the hard barrel of a gun was poked in Jim's ribs. Slowly they went ahead, and after what seemed like an eternity, they came again to the rotten log. Lang himself wriggled forward, tested it with the back of his ax, then tearing loose a number of long vines, he straddled the dangerous path, hauled himself forward with the vines, and after ten breathless minutes, he dropped off at the other side and the men he had left behind, sighed with relief.

"It's solid over here," he called. Then Mills made the journey, but he did not need to loosen the vines, so it took him less time, and presently he was standing beside the leader. The Flying Buddies saw the two confer, and finally nod agreement.

"Leave them kids till next to the last," Mills ordered. Quickly the third man made his way over, then the fourth, while the fifth stood with his gun out ready to shoot if either of the boys moved.

"We can't make it with our arms tied," Jim protested.

"I don't care if you make it or not. Get on there—"

"Listen, if we don't make it, you don't, see," Bob spoke quietly.

"No?"

"No. It's this way, if the log doesn't hold us or we have to kick it much to keep on, it's going to break good and plenty, and when it breaks, it leaves you here, just like that, caught between the two traps," he explained, and the fellow's face went white as a sheet.

CHAPTER IV
GHOSTS

"Hey, what are you waiting for?" Lang called sharply.

"These kids want their arms loose," the guardian answered.

"Tell 'em to slide with their heels—"

"I won't. I gotta get over, haven't I!" The fellow's teeth chattered and the weapon he held wavered in his trembling hand.

"Send one along. I'll meet him," Mills decided.

"All right, get on, if you kick that thing I'm goin' ter pump you full of lead, and your buddy too, see." The man poked his white face into Jim's.

"Surely, it's quite clear." Jim stepped forward, straddled the log, inched himself along with the greatest care, but his heart was in his throat as bits were knocked off. He had gone almost half the distance when he saw Mills throw himself full length from the other side, and stretch out his hands.

"Bend forward." Jim did and Mills clutched his collar firmly, then wriggled back. Half an hour later Bob was over safely, but when he stood up a great hunk of the log fell away.

"Listen," he cried, "that will never hold another man, and that chap over there is scared stiff. Loosen my arms, or Jim's, then we can get him with the lariat and if he starts to fall, haul him up. He'll never make it—he's heavier than we are."

"Wait up, over there," Lang shouted.

"What for?" he snarled suspiciously. "I aint hanging round here."

"Wait up till we get a rope—" Just then a strange wailing sound came from behind the man and he glanced fearfully over his shoulder. Mills had started to remove Bob's rope, but his fingers were clumsy and he fumbled nervously.

"Hold that light closer," he growled to the chap who had the flash. The rays were directed on the knot while the rest stood impatiently watching, and after a moment one of the men laughed; it sounded like a cackle.

"Those kids—"

"What you waiting for?" called the man across the gully.

"Keep your shirt on, we're going to throw the rope—"

"Woo-oo-o-oh," came the weird sound again, only louder. It seemed to be getting closer quickly, rose from a deep moan to a shrill wail that filled the narrow passage, and the man who was holding the flash let it fall from his cold fingers.

"I'll hold it—"

"I'm coming—" roared the one on the other side. He glanced over his shoulder a second time, then the sound came nearer, louder, and more terrible. With a shriek he flung himself astride the log, his body flat, his arms and legs kicking furiously as he shoved frantically forward, disregarding the danger of the undertaking.

"Be careful," yelled Jim as he watched the fellow, whose limbs were striking out like a floundering swimmer, sending a shower of rotten timber to the depths below. "Take it easy, you won't make any headway."

"Look out—" Mills stopped his futile efforts to get the rope, Lang turned the rays of the light on the log, while one of the other men stood astride the end trying to swing a long vine to the hands of their comrade. He bent forward and threw the long twining end, but the chap was not looking at him, the bit of tendril brushed his cheek; and with a howl of panic he twisted about desperately.

"Catch it," Lang shouted.

"Get a hold," Mills added. But the man was too terrified to understand. With a wild lunge he threw himself on the weakest part of the log, clawed with both hands, sending a shower of chips into the abyss and at the same time, the awful unearthly cry came again. Another panic-stricken lunge, the log creaked dismally, parted in the middle, and dropped its burden to the depths. The fellow who was astride the end was nearly taken with it, but Mills caught and hauled him to safety.

"If he'd waited for the rope he could have been saved," Bob said softly, and there was genuine regret in his tone. It was a tragic situation, standing tied helplessly while a fellow human fell to his death.

"Something's back there—"

"I believe that is only wind," Jim declared.

"Wind, how do you make that out?"

"Since the air purified, either there is a high wind outside or something happened to let in a good breeze. It played on those tight streamers and vines like a harp—"

"Queer harp," Mills muttered with a shiver.

"Just the same, that's all it is, I'm sure. If you have been around the Andes much, you've heard something like it before—"

"Well, I haven't been, and I'm getting out now fast as I can, see?"

"Come on," Lang ordered, and putting Jim in front to lead the way, they started forward again, but now there were only four members of the gang with the Buddies.

The way was wide enough so that they could go side by side, and although their shoulders touched as they proceeded, they did not exchange a word, for Mills and Lang were right behind them. After all, it did not make much difference, but there was really nothing to say. The queer noise was repeated at intervals, but although it was terrifying enough, the men grew less fearful of it and seemed to accept Austin's explanation as to its origin. The boy had thought it was the wind when he first heard it, but had kept silent partly because his opinion was not asked and partly because he felt that the bandits deserved a good scare. He reasoned that if they were frightened they might be less vicious in their dealings with their captives, but when he saw the havoc it was creating he endeavored to reassure them. However, if any of them appreciated his assistance no sign was made of the fact, and the pair were urged to proceed ahead.

"If there is danger they figure we'll get it first," Bob whispered, and Jim nodded.

"These kids are terribly slow," snapped a man in the rear. "We want to get out of this place."

"Sure, Lang, hurry 'em up," said the other nervously. "This hole is spooky. Why in blazes didn't you find out what was in it?"

"Shut up, I'm managing this," Lang snapped back.

"If them kids has a pull with the Indians they'll get us through," Mills called, and then the Buddies understood that the leaders expected to share any protection that the presence of the "Don's little pets" as he called them, might be to the gang. This was a phase neither of the boys had thought of, and now they exchanged swift glances.

"We're going along nice now; when Red was leading it was tough," added Lang, then went on to Bob, who had stared back. "Your help is appreciated a lot you can see, but any funny business and you'll wish you had dropped over off the log with Red."

"You said we'd be out of here in a few minutes. It's getting worse instead of better," the rear man grumbled.

"Yeh, it's thick and hot. My light won't last forever. Got any more batteries?"

"Yes." They paused to fix the flash, and Lang swore at them roundly. "I told you to have new lights, and to pack spare fillers. What did you mean by coming half ready—"

"Aw shut up, my light was brand new, but Red carried the extras," the other admitted reluctantly. At that Lang and Mills ripped out a string of oaths.

"Haul in," one snapped finally. "Didn't you tell us to divide the stuff—well, Red took the batteries—that's that—"

"And we'll likely have to crawl out of this in the dark, land somewhere in the forest, and who knows how we'll get back to the machines?" Mills thundered. "What are you carrying?"

"Grub," came the answer.

"Well, let's stop and eat. We can make better time when we are not so empty," Lang proposed. "Pass it along." He and Lang sat down as best they could in the narrow quarters with only the smallest light to pierce the gloom which surrounded them. The Buddies also let their feet slide from under them and were grateful for the opportunity to rest. The two men who brought up the rear showed no such disposition, but stepped forward over the other's legs.

"Here," the last one muttered, dropping what looked like a paper bag into Lang's lap, then went on quickly. The leader started to open the container, then glanced up with a scowl.

"Where's the rest of the stuff?" he demanded.

"Think we been traveling for hours with nothing in our stomachs?" came the answer.

"What's left?" Mills snapped, grabbing the bag.

"Aw there's a couple of sandwiches en a hard boiled egg—"

Mills sprang to his feet but the pair jumped out of his way quickly.

"Come on, Mills, eat what there is," Lang called, so the tall man returned, and the two soon devoured the frugal repast. Not a bite was offered to the Buddies whose food had been left in the plane on the hill, and whose stomachs were clamoring furiously. Presently the meal was finished to the last crumb, then the leaders rose to their feet. They did haul their companions up so they could stand, then without a word, gave them a shove forward.

Slowly and painfully the four proceeded. The Flying Buddies' feet hurt with every step, and their tired bodies wavered from side to side as they went on and on. By that time they were going through what appeared to be a grassy section of the forest. The passage wound among huge trees, over piles of fallen timber, then, suddenly from ahead, they heard a wild shriek of terror, followed by a series of shrill earsplitting screams.

"Good Heavens, what they got into?" Lang panted.

"Get on," Mills urged. He slipped his hand under Bob's arm and helped him forward, while Jim and Lang stumbled along as quickly as possible. Presently they came to a section where piles of rotten vegetation lined both sides of the route, and by the dim light Lang cast ahead, they made out one body lying still, while the other battled furiously with some hissing object that lashed and struck with thunderous blows.

"Snakes," Bob whispered.

They saw a second man borne down to the ground and after a convulsive struggle for a moment, he too lay still. The four stopped horrified in their tracks. For minutes they stood staring too paralyzed to go forward or back, then Bob saw the great snakes slide off to one side and disappear under the debris.

"Come on, walk carefully and be quick," he panted, and started to run, forcing his aching feet to carry him on. Passing the spot they could see that their two companions had probably stumbled over the reptiles, angered them to instant attack, and were utterly defenseless against the poisonous brutes.

Hardly daring to breathe lest the snakes come out again, the four tiptoed forward, but in each hand of the leaders were small, deadly guns ready to destroy the snakes if they showed their heads. Beads of perspiration stood out on the four faces, and for the first time since they started, Lang neglected to keep an eye on the captives. Half an hour later the place was well behind them and they were traversing a sandy way which took them to a stream.

"I've got to have a drink," Jim declared, and without further ado, he dropped flat and buried his face in the cool depths.

Caldwell followed his example, and soon Mills and Lang were also stretched full length and drinking deeply.

"Maybe it's poison but I don't care," Mills muttered.

"Better not take too much at a time," Jim warned. "Drink a little, then rest and drink some more." The suggestion was carried out. Several times they did it, then, with a sigh, Mills rolled over and closed his eyes.

"Hey, Mills, what's the matter with you?" Lang shook him roughly by the shoulder.

"Dog tired," he answered. "I'm going to sleep."

"Sure that water didn't knock you out?" Lang persisted fearfully.

"It's grand water. I'm going to sleep beside it, have some more when I wake up, then go on," he said heavily.

"So'm I," Lang declared, but he took the precaution to tie the ends of the ropes which bound the arms of the Flying Buddies to separate trees so that they could not help each other to get away, then he, too, closed his eyes. Jim watched him several minutes, the smallest flash light in one hand, a gun in the other. The boy thought that he could keep awake and that he and his buddy could make some plan, but his own lids grew heavy and presently all of them were sound asleep, in spite of the terrors which surrounded them.

It seemed to Austin as if he had barely closed his eyes when he felt something brush gently against his cheek and instantly he was wide awake. The first thing he noticed was the dim light sending its feeble ray into the darkness, cutting a faint glow which made the rest of the place blacker. The boy tried to brush his face on his shoulder, which ached woefully but as far as he could see or feel there was nothing near him. Mills snored melodiously, while the deep breathing of the other two could be heard plainly, but no other sound broke the death-like stillness of the ancient passage.

"Reckon I'm so tired and sore I'm imagining things," he told himself, then glanced across to where Caldwell was huddled like himself close to a tree. The boy closed his eyes again, but a moment later they were wide open, so he shifted his position quietly and began to try to make a plan which would help them get away. Carefully he moved his face about the ground hoping to discover a sharp stone upon which he might rub the rope until it was cut in two, but he found nothing, then he began to hitch and wriggle his body. It was a mighty painful process for his arms were swollen and he dared not make a sound. At last, after a grim struggle, he had the satisfaction of feeling the lariat shove upward toward his shoulders. If he could get it as high as his neck he would be free. With a heart pounding hopefully he persisted. Twice he had to stop precious minutes for Lang stirred in his sleep and the lad feared he would wake and discover what he was doing. Nearly an hour passed and at last the rope was slipped above his shoulders; a moment more and he was out of it.

All this while his mind was working like a trip hammer planning what to do when he got loose. The first thing would be to take possession of Lang's gun. With that in his pocket he might force the men to release Bob in case he wasn't able to do it himself. His step-brother was the other side of Mills and whether that journey could be made safely was another matter. With the weapon in his pocket at last, Jim devoted the next few minutes to rubbing his sore arms, for he knew that in their present condition he could never hold the gun, much less fire it effectively. In due time his arms were relieved, then he wished that he had on soft-soled shoes, but he managed to get to his feet, take possession of the flash-light, and at last, assured that his activities were unobserved, he made his way to Bob's side, bending over him carefully. Instantly the young fellow looked up in startled surprise, then Jim grinned, for Bob was industriously chewing his own rope and had managed to get half way through it. A moment more and it was cut and he too was free, while Jim took Mills' gun, which he gave to the younger boy.

"This place is lighter," Bob whispered, and Jim glanced around. He was greatly puzzled, for as far as he could see there was no explanation to the fact. No one seemed to be coming with a light and certainly no new opening had been made into the passage, but the glow was unmistakable and it filled the place. Gently Jim rubbed his step-brother's body, and presently, Bob stood up, but just then Mills stirred uneasily, so the Sky Buddies sat down again quickly and quietly. They watched through half closed eyes, and although Mills tossed restlessly, he finally lay still and again his melodious snore broke the silence.

"Grand uproar," Bob grinned. Then he got busy knotting his rope, and looped it on his arm. "We'll do a bit of tying," he announced.

"Wait," Jim whispered, then he motioned his pal to move further from the sleepers. They stopped several feet away. "I have an idea. Suppose we lay the ropes so when they sit up we'll have them hog-tied with a loop, and as soon as we're ready we'll wake them and make them get moving."

"Good idea," Bob agreed. "They had something to eat and some sleep, and we didn't. Got any of those pellets Ynilea gave you—"

"You bet, I forgot all about them." Jim fished the tiny container of food pellets they had been given at the laboratory, and the pair soon had some in their mouths.

"Look," Bob pointed along the way they had come and to their astonishment they saw a young girl carrying a basket on her head. She came toward them as if unconscious of their presence, her sandaled feet hardly touching the floor of the passage, her body covered with a whole tiger-skin. Behind her walked a woman, then several men came forward single file. Every one of them carried boxes, some opened and others closed, while a few older men carried bags woven of grass. The band came closer and closer until the girl passed directly in front of the Buddies. She never turned her dark eyes but went on, stepping over the sleepers.

"Natives," Jim whispered.

Both of them completely forgot to lay the lariats, which were looped in their left hands, then suddenly an exclamation made them whirl about. Lang was sitting up rubbing his eyes stupidly, while Mills too was staring wide awake.

CHAPTER V
THE WAY OUT

The bandits sat up, stared with mouths gaping at the band of Indians filing silently past them. Neither Mills nor Lang appeared to realize that the captives had managed to free themselves of the ropes, and the Flying Buddies, the small guns resting ready in their palms, were on the alert, prepared to turn the tables on the men if necessary.

In the meantime the entire passage was illuminated with a weird yellow light and the natives' moving bodies cast grotesque shadows before, behind and all about them. Huge dark figures out of all proportion, wavered through the narrow cavern as they, completely ignoring the presence of the white men, passed along soundlessly. It was a strange spectacle the lads witnessed, and one they could not explain. There were about forty or fifty men, women and young girls, all carrying precious burdens in ancient receptacles, and occasionally a glittering object fell from the over-flowing containers. One of these dropped between Lang's knees and his eyes glowed greedily as they rested on it, but he sat with eyes and mouth open and did not move.

For ten or fifteen minutes the strange procession passed slowly along and finally the last man, a tall young Indian armed with a long, black-tipped spear, brought up the rear. He paused for an instant beside Mills, and stared down at the man who crouched in terror, then he proceeded to join his companions. He was out of sight before Lang leaped to his feet. In his hand was the jewel which had fallen, and his face was contorted with viciousness.

"Mills, it's native—"

"Think I'm blind," Mills muttered, but he got up more slowly; it was not easy to rid himself of the effect of those dark piercing eyes.

"They are carrying away tons of stuff; gold and stones. We hit the place all right. Come on, we'll see where they hide it and help ourselves—" Lang was nearly consumed with excitement.

"Help ourselves—" Mills repeated dully.

"Sure, look!" He held out the shining trinket. "Those natives always do that, I've read about it. Years ago—they hid carloads of stuff and nobody could find it, but lately some caches have been located and these fellows are hiding their treasures in a new place. We'll see where it is—"

"Say, Bo, listen, we aint awake, see! This is a dream I'm havin', all by myself, you aint in it at all, but you seem to be." Mills brushed his hand over his forehead.

"Oh, you're crazy," Lang insisted.

"Just asleep. We been thinkin' so much about those hiding places that I'm dreaming all this, but listen, if it was real those fellows would never have trailed right over us like that— never—why, I could see right through them—it's a dream I tell you—"

"Come along, I'll show you if it's a dream," Lang shouted. "They'll get away if we don't hustle." He dashed off after the last Indian who had disappeared from sight.

Mills followed reluctantly at a slower pace, while the Flying Buddies cautiously brought up the rear. As he went on they could hear him muttering to himself that he was dreaming, that it wasn't real, and Lang was a nut.

"It does seem queer," Bob remarked thoughtfully.

"Shall I give you a pinch so you'll be sure you are awake?" Jim asked soberly.

"Yes, go ahead," Caldwell invited. His step-brother started to comply but he no sooner got a bit of the fleshy part of his arm between his fingers than Bob drew away. "I'm convinced. Come on, hurry up, it isn't as light as it was!"

The pellets the boys had swallowed some hours earlier had refreshed them amazingly so they forgot that they had had little food, rest or water, as they ran as hard as they could go along the passage, which presented no difficulties to progress. They had raced about five minutes before they overtook Lang and Mills, and some distance ahead they could see the backs of the Indians marching forward with dignified tread. Nearly a quarter of an hour the white men followed the dark ones through the opening in the dense forest until at last Lang, who was leading, paused and raised his hand. Mills drew close to his partner, but the Flying Buddies remained at a respectful distance. They were on higher ground and could see quite easily what was happening.

The place beyond where the Buddies were standing was like a deep gully whose sides rose steeply, like a wall. Thick vines grew about twenty feet from the bottom and these were woven across the top in an impenetrable mass through which neither rain nor sunshine could pass. The boxes and baskets were placed on the ground in a circle and the men stood behind them, each armed with long and short spears. It looked as if the women were moving about preparing a meal, but suddenly there came a fierce braying of dogs, the thunder of galloping hoofs, hundreds of them, and the deafening clatter of steel. A moment later a huge black brute with powerful hungry jaws leaped in from behind the rocks, and almost instantly a horse and rider raced furiously in after him.

"Great Guns, Bob, he's in armor," Jim whispered.

"Bronc and all," Caldwell added in amazement. It reminded the boys of some historical moving picture in which armored knights and horses suddenly leaped to life and action. For a breathless instant they stood too astonished to speak.

After their leader, a great pack of the dogs rushed along with soldiers protected from head to foot by their coats of mail and helmets. Queer weapons were fired, blunderbusses and heavy cross-bows, long swords flashed and after ten minutes of the wildest confusion the natives were dead, all except a few women and children who were slung up behind the soldiers, while others gathered the treasure in their arms and galloped away with the rich booty, but as they scrambled up the rocks, a number of them were dislodged and came tumbling down. The stones seemed to mark the wall of some natural dam, for instantly there was a terrific boom, boom, and tons of water roared over, sweeping the burdened horses helplessly before it. Snarling and fighting the dogs struggled to swim to safety, but most of them were battered by heavy armor or kicking hoofs, so that they sunk with their laden masters in the swirling water.

"Get back," Lang shrieked in terror, but although the water had reached their side, the main part of it found a lower outlet, and it flowed off among the boulders. However it was deep enough so that there was no evidence of what it concealed, and the four who had witnessed the horrible tragedy stared mutely at one another.

"I tell you I'm dreaming," Mills repeated.

"Let's get out of here," cried Lang, glancing about him fearfully.

"How are we going to do it?"

"Follow the stream around to the other side," Jim suggested.

"Say, what in—"

"You needn't say it," Jim snapped, or rather barked. "Face about and get going. Make it lively—"

"You brats—"

"Save those little pleasantries for later, old man," Jim ordered. "It's your turn to lead this party—"

"I'll be killed—"

"Surely," Bob cut in. "You'll get what you promised us if you don't do as you are told. The first thing is to relieve yourself of your weapons, all of them. Turn your pockets inside out, both of you."

"Well—"

"Don't wait." Bob pressed forward, the gun pointing straight at Mills' belt and in terror the fellow threw up his hands. "I told you to turn your pockets inside out, and take off your gun belt. Do it quick or I'll shoot it off. My folks taught me to use a gun when they showed me how to handle a spoon, and right now I've got a lot against you; my fingers are itching to press the spring, besides it would be no end easier for Buddy and me to get out of this place alone. We're only taking you along because we like your company—"

"We'd better tie them up and leave them here," Jim suggested, although he had no such intention.

"Don't do that—don't do that—" Lang's teeth chattered with fright as he pleaded, and he hastily turned his pockets wrong side out, also removed his cartridge belt and a holster which he had strapped under his arm. Jim kicked the stuff into the water, while Bob attended to Mills.

"Now, take off your shirts then we'll be sure you haven't got anything hidden or try anything queer. I'm going to tie you, but not so that you are as helpless as we were." While Jim stood guard, he secured the pair with the one lariat, then he took the end of the rope. "Just a little funny business and this will pull up tight, so watch yourself—now goose-step."

The two men faced about and started, Caldwell holding one end of their rope. He had the gun in his other hand, while Jim walked beside him, his weapon pointed at the bare backs. It was difficult making their way along the edge of the stream, but they finally managed it, then saw that the route lead forward in a comparatively smooth trail. Two hours they proceeded, winding in and out, twisting and turning as if the designers of the passage had sought to build a labyrinth for some ancient lover's lane. Then the way grew suddenly quite rugged and a bit later the boys and their captured captors discovered that they were tramping over a high stone bridge which seemed to be a natural formation of the rocks. All of the time the vines and trees formed the solid arch above their heads, but occasionally sections were considerably lighter than others.

"Say, where do you think you are going to take us?" Mills growled.

"Out," Bob answered shortly.

"Yeh, when we get out, then what?"

"To the nearest jail, where you belong," Jim told him.

"Well, I'm telling you now, I'm not going to no jail," Mills cried.

"Aw shut up," Lang ordered.

"Shut up yourself," Mills retorted. "I aint done nothing to go to jail for—"

"No, well you've done as much as I have—"

"You're a liar." Mills fist shot out and he struck his companion a resounding crack on the side of the face.

Lang's foot went up hard, caught the fellow in the stomach with such force that Mills doubled up like a jackknife, screamed with pain, and his feet slipped so that he slid across the rock.

"Catch him, Lang," Jim shouted quickly.

"He'll take you with him," warned Bob.

At that the gang leader clutched the rope which held the two but Mills was already dangling over the edge. Desperately Lang threw all his weight on the opposite side. Jim and Bob sprang to help him, but as they pulled the section of the rope which Caldwell had knotted after he had chewed the strands, parted, and the smaller man went tumbling over backward into the rushing stream. The boys dared not stop to help him, but put all their strength into dragging Mills to safety. It was minutes before the big man was on the bridge again, and by that time there was no sign of the leader of the gang, although the boys made every effort to locate him. They were panting from the exertion and pale with horror at what had happened.

"Can you walk now?" Jim asked grimly.

"Yes," Mills answered.

"We'll be on our way." Silently they proceeded and just beyond the next turn they found themselves in the ruins of an ancient court with moss-grown stone seats which faced the east.

"Looks a bit like one of the temple ruins near Cuzco," Caldwell remarked just to make conversation.

"Yes," replied Austin, then added with a sigh of relief, "Jinks, Buddy, the sun is shining through! Isn't it great!"

"Surely is," Bob agreed. They looked about and although some of the larger branches of the tall trees interlaced over their heads, the foliage was not so matted and they were sure that either no attempt had been made by the natives to conceal the spot, or any ancient hiding growths had been broken away during the passing years. Mills glanced nervously around him and when he saw that they were really in the sunlight, he began to babble incoherently.

"Think we'd better let him go?" Jim suggested. There was pity in his tone and he spoke softly for he thought that this last member of the gang that had taken them prisoners was losing what little reason he ever possessed.

"I figure we're out of the passage, but we don't know where we are yet. If we turn him loose he may starve to death before he reaches a settlement or any one runs across him; then, if we let him keep with us until we get out it will be safer to keep him in hand. He can be a nasty bird and after a while some of the effects of what we were through may wear off, then he'll revert to his charming self again and probably try to break our necks," Bob answered, and after a moment's consideration, Jim nodded that it was the wiser course.

"Go along," he motioned to Mills, whose knees wobbled under him and his fingers fumbled inanely about his mouth.

"He's nutty, all right," said Bob.

They advanced toward the towering ruin, and crossed what had once been a magnificent Square with a beautiful fountain playing in the centre. The clear water still trickled up between the stones, some of which were polished until they glistened like fiery opals. The other side of the square was the first tier of a wide terrace, its massive walls seamed in even lines as its ancient builders had laid the rocks with infinite care, one above the other, and side by side. There were a few small fruit trees whose branches were gnarled and twisted; several giant olives which might have been imported from Spain hundreds of years ago; tall cactus with thorns sharp as spear points and strong as spikes stuck up like sentinels, while patches of smaller varieties spread over large sections of the sandy soil.

The Buddies and their half-witted companion made their way slowly around where they could walk safely and presently they discovered a groove. They were not sure if it had once been the bed of a small stream or a path worn through the years by the natives whose abodes had been somewhere in the vicinity, but they followed it because it was easier walking and soon they reached an irregular, winding stairway with a high, stone balustrade on both sides.

"Let's go up as far as we can," Jim proposed.

"That's a good idea. From the top we may be able to get our bearings," Bob assented. He was usually full of fun despite adventures or danger, but the long hours spent in the passage, the tragic events which had piled themselves one after the other, had left him grave. There wasn't a sign of a grin on his lips, and his usually laughing eyes were mighty thoughtful.

"Hope we can find a way to the plane soon," said Jim as they proceeded upward.

"Me too," Bob replied, then he glanced about. "I say, Buddy, the sun is where it was when we started in that passage."

"I was thinking of that," Jim told him. They stopped and looked at each other.

"Suppose we were there more than one round of the clock?"

"I don't believe so. It's a safe bet we were there twenty-four hours, or nearly. I was depending on the plane clock, so didn't wear a watch."

"Red cribbed mine when he was searching me," Bob said quietly.

"Eh, why didn't you tell him it was a relation of the green emerald rings?" Jim chuckled. "Mills was certainly afraid of them."

"I thought of that, but I should worry. Gosh, Red surely—"

"Here we are on a second terrace," Jim interrupted for he wanted Bob to forget, as fast as he could, that experience at the rotten log where Red had met his fate.

"Must have been a wonderful structure this," Bob answered. He understood why Jim had cut in, and was as anxious as the older boy to get the troubles of the last twenty-four hours out of his mind.

"Seems to me I hear something, a sort of tapping," said Jim. They stood still and listened, every nerve tense, but gradually they relaxed for the place was as silent as the bottom of the deepest unopened tomb in the universe.

"Hear it now?"

"Guess it was my imagination. Come on." They started again, crossed the second terrace, and several times they paused to scan the sky. In fact, they were far more interested in what might come out of the path of the blazing sun than what they would discover on terra-firma, for they both felt confident that their absence had not passed unobserved by their friends at the barracks.

"Figuring that we tramped twelve or fifteen hours all together, how many miles do you believe we covered?" Jim asked when they stopped to rest on the third terrace.

"Sometimes we went pretty slowly," Bob answered.

"I know. I was trying to dope it out as we went along. It didn't seem to me as if the passage made many turns, but that's hard to tell because it went up and down, across rivers and probably under sections of the mountains."

"Sure, but it seems to me we can't be as much as a hundred miles from the top of that little hill, where we started. To be sure, it wasn't very high, but for natives to have a covered way—gosh—I don't know. We did hear that the ancient natives made hidden ways for hundreds of miles; they needed to in order to get away, but it doesn't seem possible that we can have gone a hundred miles—"

"Anyway, we can't be a hundred air miles from where we started. What I'm trying to figure is the chances of Bradshaw and some of the rest locating us soon."

"Yes, they'll be hunting sure as fate but I'm afraid even if they flew over that place where the planes were left, they would not notice them. Those lads did a good job of covering up."

"That's right—"

"Jim, shhh—there's somebody, a white man, sneaking behind those rocks just ahead of us," Bob whispered softly.

CHAPTER VI
AN OLD ENEMY APPEARS

His Flying Buddy's announcement that he saw some one stealing about the ancient ruin was made in such a startled tone, that Austin, for a moment was deeply mystified. They had been through such a ghastly experience that their minds were not functioning normally, and both of them were instantly on the alert for additional danger. For a minute the three stood still, Mills indifferently, but the boys alert and watchful, then suddenly Jim began to think more rationally and he drew a deep breath of relief.

"It's probably some one looking for us," he declared. "Let's go along and catch up with him." But Bob caught his sleeve.

"Put on the curb, Old Timer, it isn't anyone looking for us," he insisted. "Come on, let's lean against the wall as if we are resting and see what we can see. Keep your gun where it will do the most good in the shortest time." He stepped leisurely across to the section of wall, and leaned back wearily, while his step-brother also assumed an attitude of fatigue, because he wanted to get more information, not because he was convinced that whoever was about was not a friend.

"What did he look like?"

"Couldn't tell much. He's wearing a grey suit, or a dirty white one, and a dark straw hat. I saw him the first time when we crossed the Square. He was up among those trees and I thought it was some kind of wild animal, then I saw him again when we were coming up the stairs from the lower terrace. My first idea was that it was a friend, I was going to shout, but he dodged back out of sight. When I saw him this last time, he was peeking from behind those stones as if he was watching to see which way we are headed. I do not believe he knows I saw him," Bob said so softly that Jim barely caught the words.

"Gosh—sure it isn't a native—you know they do hang around these ruins and it may be that he is put here to look out for the temple."

"It isn't a native. The ones who are not in the towns are all strong and straight looking and they don't wear white men's clothing," replied Bob. They remained as they were carefully considering their next step, and as they stood thinking, their eyes rested on Mills who was crouching at the end of the rope very much like a monkey on a string.

"He's surely off his bean," Jim remarked, and Bob nodded his head.

"Suppose we saunter around, and get as high on this ruin as we can so we can see as far as possible. That's the most important thing we have to do," he said.

"Yes. Instead of taking the side we have been following, let's go to the left. If the snooper is really spying on us we can tell quickly enough. If he isn't, he'll go about his business," Jim proposed.

"That's good sense. If we find out he's all right, of course we might get some information about getting out of these woods."

"Yes, and when we get way up we'd bet-[Transcriber's note: missing text at this point in several copies of the original book.]

"We'll have to do it Indian fashion; by rubbing sticks, then we can direct a column that will rise high and show airmen, who are sure to be looking for us, where we are located."

"That's our best bet. Knocks the spots off roaming about the forest in a circle, besides I expect they are so thick in these parts that even a signal fire would not help us. Come along, Mills. Gee, I feel like a blooming organ grinder. Keep eyes ahead and behind."

"Atta boy. Don't give up the ship."

The pair started single file with Mills going with them either on all fours or with his legs doubled and his hands fumbling about his mouth. His imbecility was uncanny and the boys would have liked nothing better than to be rid of him, but neither of them thought of deserting the helpless man even though his presence added to their danger and the difficulties they must face. Leisurely they proceeded across the terrace opposite the direction they had first taken, and although they appeared to pay little attention to the great structure they were traveling, their eyes and ears were alert. They reached the stairway, which was higher and narrower than the lower ones, but as they neared the top, it curved wide and brought them to an enormous circular platform. Here they paused and stood taking in the strange, wild scene.

Behind the boys were two more terraces which appeared larger than those they had ascended, while in front of them stretched the ruins of the once flourishing city which had been built with amazing skill in the shadow of the Temple. Here and there giant stones remained standing defiantly in spite of centuries of storms, winds and rains; and in spite of destructive hands which had sought to tear them from their foundations. A slight breeze was blowing. Just enough to make the cactus creak and crackle; dead grasses rustled softly, slender trees swayed slightly, the leaves of the stronger ones waved like beckoning hands as if they would recall the lost wonders of the past.

"I hear that tapping again," Jim whispered. They listened for a moment and then Caldwell also heard the sound.

"It might be a woodpecker," he remarked.

"We might believe that if our snooping friend had not shown himself," said Jim. "Seems to be on the further side. Let's try to work around on the further side, but first we best get higher and build that fire. Wonder if there is any wood up there."

"Reckon there must be. This sure is the sort of place that makes one feel creepy; the place and Mills together are enough to give a fellow the heaves. Seems to me I smell something to eat—" They sniffed the air and as the breeze was coming toward them they made out the fragrance of bacon being toasted.

"Guess our friend is going to eat—" Just then Mills tugged on the rope, he raised himself to his full height, his nostrils expanding as he breathed deeply.

"He must be empty as a drum. Wonder if it would be safe to feed him one of those pellets—I—" But the sentence was not finished. With a wild leap, Mills broke away, tore furiously up the nearest stairway and disappeared at an astonishing rate of speed over the higher terrace.

"We must go after him, but keep your gun handy."

The Sky Buddies ran as fast as their legs could carry them, but they both knew that Mills was setting a much swifter pace. When they reached the next terrace they caught a glimpse of the top of his head as he descended in unhuman bounds, and without a word, the pals ran after him. Across the terrace they found, instead of stairs, that the madman had gone by way of a rugged trail, partly overgrown with brush. As they leaped after him, in sections they had to hang on to the tough shrubs, but as far as they could see, Mills rushed on without assistance and completely ignoring the fact that a false step would send him tumbling on the giant rocks below.

"Watch out," Jim warned as he suddenly realized they would have to round a bend close to the wall. Cautiously they proceeded, and in a moment they were on a small artificially built ledge which looked as if it might have been meant for some sort of observation post, for from its height was a wide open stretch over the city, and when the woods beyond were less dense, a guard might have been able to see for miles. Here the boys had to stop for they could get no further, but Mills was nowhere in sight.

"Great guns, he must have been going so fast he went right over," Bob gasped, but Jim lay flat, wriggled to the edge and looked down. "Is he dead?"

"No." Austin moved back and whispered. "He's all right, but it's a wonder he isn't smashed to a pulp. Reckon he had a sort of bump for he's leaning against the wall."

"See anyone else?"

"No. Keep quiet."

Bob joined his step-brother and presently the boys were staring down at the man who had escaped from them. He appeared a bit dazed, then suddenly he started up vigorously and proceeded along the narrow way toward a row of high stones which looked as if they might once have been a part of the great wall, but now they were standing irregularly several inches apart. At first the boys could see no one else, then close to the far edge of the terrace they made out a tiny wreath of smoke as if some one had built a small fire.

"That's where the smell of cooking comes from," Bob whispered.

"I suppose the thought of food is what started Mills off like mad—gee—wonder where—oh there he is." Another white man stepped unsuspectingly from between the rocks, stood an instant as if expecting a companion, then he scooped something from the fire and prepared to eat.

"Can't wait for his company," Bob grinned. "If we hadn't eaten those pellets we'd know exactly how empty Mills must be."

"Yes, and I was just thinking of feeding him one. We'd better not watch here too closely, we don't want to be taken by surprise from above or behind."

"You bet," Bob agreed.

"That chap is wearing some sort of dark suit, Buddy."

"I see, so there must be two here. This can't be the one who was watching us," answered Bob.

"Which means that the other fellow knows, or will know in a few minutes just where we have taken ourselves. You see what's going on down there and I'll be ready to stem any rear attack," proposed Jim.

"That's O.K. with me, but don't go off anywhere, we don't want to get separated, not an inch," Bob insisted.

"I won't," Jim promised. He placed himself so that he could see the section which curved and not forgetting to watch above, he stood guard while Bob stretched out again. Austin rather expected they would discover this was some friendly woodsman or hunter who would show them how to get through the forest or to their plane, but in Bob's mind there wasn't a doubt as to the attitude of the persons occupying the ancient temple ruin.

Now the young fellow determined to see what was happening on the edge of the terrace and be thoroughly convinced of the kindliness of the stranger before he made any advance. The man he saw appeared to be consuming sandwiches and baked potatoes and as he devoured them he walked up and down as if anxious to finish. Twice he went beyond the boy's range of vision and came back stamping his feet angrily. Caldwell was so interested in watching the stranger that he nearly forgot Mills, but presently he saw that worthy crouched and moving stealthily forward, dodging from stone or shrub toward the fire.

"Poor fellow, he must be terribly hungry. Perhaps when he gets something to eat and drink he'll get over his craziness," was Bob's mental comment. He felt sorry for Mills, but there was something so menacing in that slinking figure that he was almost tempted to shout a warning to the stranger. However, when he thought of it soberly, Mills was weakened by the hour's experience, the long steady tramp without food he reasoned would not make him a very dangerous antagonist. He wanted something to eat and the boy could not imagine anyone refusing to give him food.

"Anything interesting?" Jim whispered.

"No. See the other chap?" Bob asked.

"Not yet."

Their tasks were resumed and by that time Caldwell saw the stranger walking away from his fire. He seemed to have appeased his own appetite, but he did not put out the blaze, merely piled coals over it, left some sort of cooking utensil near by, then started briskly toward the great stones which were all that remained of that section of the edifice. His jaws were working vigorously and in his hand was a hunk of bread and meat which he doubtless determined to consume as he went. The boy wondered what he was doing in the locality, then suddenly he thought there was something familiar about that striding figure. He stared an instant longer as the man drew closer, then he gave a soft whistle.

"What is it?" Jim whispered. Bob sat up, or rather wriggled back.

"Take a good look at that lad," he said, "I'll watch here." They exchanged places, and Jim scowled when his eyes rested on the hurrying man. "Ever see him before?"

"Surely," Jim answered excitedly.

"The thoughtful lad who carted the gas to the plane when we were on the Island coming down with your dad?"

"I'll say so," Jim answered. He distinctly remembered the day in Montego when he had gone to the little town to purchase extra gas. A group of children had been tormenting a hunch-back but had been stopped in the midst of their sport by a military-looking chap who had vanquished them in short order by the effective use of his cane. Later, the seemingly kindly man had volunteered to cart the heavy cans in his automobile to where the plane was roosting. He was most cordial and obliging, but the Flying Buddies later discovered that he had secretly brought not only the gas but the powerful dwarf, who stowed away in the "Lark" when he got a chance. Hours later, when they were over the Caribbean Sea, he attacked them viciously. Jim had been the one who fought and finally sent the rascal off the "Lark" but it had been one experience he expected he should never forget, and now he was staring at the man who had made such a villainous attempt to prevent Mr. Austin from reaching Cuzco. The recollection made him shudder and he wondered how the fellow happened to be in this particular section of the globe.

"He won't be a friend of ours," Jim said softly.

"Reckon he lost a bunch of money by not getting his little scheme through, so, if he should happen to discover us we're out of luck."

"And how!"

"Reckon we'd better leave Mills and get away from here as fast and as far as we can. Shouldn't like to run into that lad— he'd be mighty ugly and we'd have no choice but to use the guns and not miss." They both glanced over again, and then caught their breaths sharply.

The man from Montego had stopped in his tracks, while Mills, suddenly appeared in front of him. The insane fellow's hand shot out, he grabbed the food, stuffed it into his mouth ravenously, but instead of realizing how desperately hungry he was, the Montegoean furiously resented losing his meal and landed a resounding punch on Mills' head. While he used one hand for the food, Mills grabbed the other by the front of his shirt, backed him as easily as if he had been a small boy, toward his own fire. Twice he planted kicks in the other's legs, and his powerful hand was twisting the cloth tightly about his throat. Desperately the fellow tried to free himself, kicked and struck with his hands, then suddenly he filled the air with shrill shrieks of terror, but these were promptly choked off and he was backed more swiftly. In an incredibly short space of time they were both at the edge of the cliff, then Mills raised his victim, shook him as if he were a rat, then with a powerful punch, hurled him out into space.

Something went flying over the Buddies' heads and they glanced up in time to see a small figure rushing down among the rocks. He did not appear to notice the boys, but raced recklessly over the steep incline, leaped down the wall, and leaped like a mad animal across the terrace. The commotion he made seemed to pass unobserved by Mills, who was calmly raking the fire and helping himself to the food which had been left.

"Great Scott, that's the dwarf," Bob exclaimed, and sure enough the twisted figure was even more unmistakable than his master.

The dwarf leaped at Mills, who rose just as the rush was made, but his feet were planted firmly, well apart. He did not permit his meal to be interrupted by the attack, but caught the little man much as he had the bigger one. However, instead of hurling him over the cliff, he spread him out face down on the ground and proceeded to sit on him. The dwarf struggled, kicked, bit and screamed but his efforts were futile.

"I've read that an insane man has the strength of half a dozen sometimes," Jim said softly.

"Looks as if it's true," Bob answered.

"One thing is certain, we have to thank Mills for bringing our boy friend out of his hole. He must have been stalking along behind us and if it hadn't been for the fight and the yells, he'd have landed on us. That's the way I figure."

They sat quietly and had it not been for the seriousness of the situation and their own difficulty they would have indulged in a good laugh. The squirming, kicking dwarf, the undisturbed Mills pinning him to the ground while he ate a hearty meal. Finally he was satisfied, then he lifted himself, one hand clutching his victim while the other fumbled about the wriggling body. Presently he produced a cigarette and he resumed his former position while he enjoyed the smoke. He appeared rational enough and the boys were wondering whether they would be wise to go and speak to him.

"Reckon we'd better let him alone," Bob announced quite as if they had been discussing the matter.

"Gee, look!" Jim exclaimed. They saw a tall Indian striding across the terrace and presently he stood in front of Mills, who glanced up, then cringed in terror. It made the Flying Buddies think of the hour when the band had been marching with their treasure and the last man had paused to look at the bandit.

Now he touched the chap on the shoulder and the two got to their feet. Then he beckoned them to follow, which they did as if they dared not disobey. The three hurried across the terrace to the great stones, and then the boys saw the man point to the bottom of one of them. The dwarf stooped, twisted and pulled something heavy out. As nearly as they could see it was a sort of ancient strong box with a heavy cover. Mills dragged it eagerly several feet away, and then Bob clutched Jim's arm.

"That stone, look at it," he gasped. "Look out," he shouted. But it was too late. The huge stone which had been undermined groaned, tipped, then dropped forward with a mighty crash, pinning the dwarf under its tons of weight.

CHAPTER VII
THE END OF THE WAY

"Buddy, this can't be real. We must be asleep, or I must be having a nightmare," exclaimed Bob in horror as they saw the massive stone completely obliterate the dwarf.

"Old Man," Jim said shakily. "Let's call it a day and get out of here as fast as we can, but keep a grip on yourself; watch your step."

"How are we going to manage it?"

"Search me, but the thing to hang on to is the fact that we are going to make it somehow."

Bob tried to grin but it was a sickly effort, and again they glanced down at the scene below. They could see the tall Indian walking indifferently across the terrace while Mills was just getting the heavy lid off the box which had been dragged from the foundation of ancient stones. It was doubtless the removal of this support which had caused the huge thing to fall and destroy the dwarf; but the lone white man in possession of the treasure appeared to be absolutely unaffected by the tragedy. He finally succeeded in removing the cover and when it was tossed aside the sun shone brightly upon what appeared to be a wonderful collection of glittering jewels. Greedily he plunged in his hands, tossing the trinkets up as a miser might, and then he danced about the marvelous find.

"Come along," Jim caught the younger boy's sleeve and the pair turned away from the scene.

They made no comment as they climbed back to the terrace, walked thoughtfully toward the natural stairway, and at last began to climb again. On reaching the top they proceeded to the last elevation and arriving there found that it was a huge plateau which had been leveled carefully. There were several streams which ran as if they had been guided around some gardens and then the water tumbled over the edge in a sparkling fall whose spray leaped back fully twenty feet.

Taking a careful survey of their surroundings, the boys saw that to their left was a strip of woods and through the tops of the trees which were not very tall ones they could see a second clear space beyond. Between them and the clearing there was a shallow ravine which they could see grew deeper and wider as it twisted toward the ruins of the ancient city. In one place they saw a wall which had evidently been built to re-enforce the land and prevent the soil from being washed away, but in places the stone work had fallen and the action of water had left a deep, gravel wash. There was little dry timber on the site where they were making their observations and for some unexplainable reason neither of them cared to build their signal fire so near the ruined temple and its tragedies.

"Let's go a bit further back, set a course through those woods, and get on that bare place," Jim suggested.

"Suits me fine," Bob agreed. "It looks lower than this."

Without further ado they started toward the rocky ledge which rose toward the back, then, facing about prepared to make their way across the ravine through the woods. Being first class pilots they made a careful reckoning, noted several easily followed marks by which to set a course, then with a final glance around at the scene made ready to start, but before they took a step they heard a scrambling and a moment later were surprised to see Mills, laden with the heavy box, come stumbling toward them. If the man knew they were there, he made no sign, but came half stumbling along bent almost double with the weight he carried.

The boys paused uncertainly, both ready to defend themselves should the insane man attack them, but he might have been blind for all the attention he paid to them. As he drew nearer they could see his lips moving, and soon they could hear his mutterings, which were punctuated by queer crackling chuckles as if his throat was parched and dry.

"I'm awake, awake," he declared over and over. "Awake, and I have it all, every piece, millions of treasure." At that he laughed harshly, then his foot struck against a bit of projecting rock and it took all his strength to keep from falling, but he managed it, although in the balancing maneuver, the box tipped and teetered precariously. Mills jerked it tight and then a mass of the shining contents was spilled and went tumbling to the ground. "Riches, riches, and I am awake. Let it stay, let it stay—I have it all. I have it all, the others have none—I am awake and rich—rich—" The words trailed off into incoherent sounds. He made his way weakly past the boys, pieces of the treasure falling like a trail over the route, and five minutes later he disappeared in a thick grove which fringed the cliff.

"Gosh," Bob said softly when at last Mills was out of sight, "he has the treasure."

"Whew, surely." Jim stooped and picked up a handful of the fallen trinkets and as he let them fall again through his fingers, the Buddies' eyes met. Mechanically they turned their faces toward the trees which concealed their former companion.

"A box full of shells—" said Bob. "Worth four bits a ton," Jim added. "Whew, speaking of nightmares, if the sandman can beat all this adventure he's going some. Seven dead men, a crazy man, besides a band of Indians and dressed-up robbers carried away before a broken dam—whew—"

"Let's get going."

Bob kicked a cluster of the shells near his feet, then facing about resolutely, started to lead the way across the plateau, into the strip of wood, down the narrowest point of the ravine, up the other side, which was quite steep, and finally they were standing on the clear space they had picked out from the terrace. The site was bare except for a couple of rather large growths more than half way across, and the Sky Buddies noticed that it seemed to be fringed with a dense timber and long trailing vines. In every way it was an ideal location for their purpose and now they were actually away from the depressing ruins, they sighed with relief.

"We've been doing a lot of mooning around," Jim remarked cheerfully. "Let's make up for lost time."

"There's plenty of dry brush for the fire." Bob glanced into the sky, then scrutinized the heavens closely, while Jim devoted himself to getting acquainted with the vicinity. "Not a wing—" But he was interrupted by a hearty laugh which rang merrily from his step-brother's throat.

"What in the name of cat-soup and fish is the matter with you?" he demanded, but he stared at this pal anxiously. "You didn't catch anything from Mills, did you?"

"No," Jim answered, then went off again into gales of laughter. It was so loud and hearty that a sleepy echo caught it up and passed it around experimentally until it seemed as if the top of the world was indulging in a grand ha-ha-ha.

"Hey, Old Sour-dough, can it! We'll never get anything done if you indulge in hi-strikes—"

"Ha, ha, ha-ah-haa," roared Jim. Tears began to roll down his cheeks and he doubled up helplessly as he laughed.

"Ha-ha-ha," Bob repeated mechanically.

"Ha-ha-ha—" Jim kept it up and it came from his very boots.

"Say, am I so funny?" demanded Bob. He was becoming convinced that Jim's mind was badly affected by the strain of the past twenty-four hours, and he didn't wonder. "Come on, Pal, snap out of it—that won't do you any good—not a bit. Why, you are acting worse than if some one was tickling the soles of your feet—"

"I'm tickled all over," Jim gasped merrily.

"At what—be yourself or tell me what has set you off—I don't see anything to laugh at—"

"No?"

"Not a thing. This is a serious business, Old Man, we've got to keep our heads to get out of it."

"Ha-ha haaahahhhaaa," shouted Jim, then he made a slight gesture which seemed to include the entire world. "Ha-ha—"

"Ha—" Bob started to mimic him, then his eyes swept swiftly over the place. He turned himself about to look more closely, then, he too opened his mouth and roared with genuine amusement. "Ha-ha-ha-ha." It was a soul-satisfying bellow which shook him from head to foot for several minutes, then he pulled himself together. "We don't want to make any mistake." With that he ran to the nearest green pile and began to pull on it. After a moment Austin joined him, and although they continued to chuckle as they worked, they had control of themselves.

"Behold the Helicopter," Jim cried as the plane began to stand out from the covering of foliage the bandits had put on it.

"No wonder you laughed," grinned Bob.

"When I first saw it I thought I had gone crazy, then I was sure and my giggling apparatus went wide open. Gee, to think, after all that traveling—millions of miles it seemed—then to come right back to the place we started from. Gosh all Friday, it's like finding an everlasting cream puff. Whew—aint it a grand and glorious feeling!"

"I'll say! If we had built our signal fire over there on the top of the ruin and Bradshaw had found us—the plane almost under our noses, howling catnip but he would have had a laugh on us. It was a close shave all right."

"Suppose I go over the machine and you take a look at the other one. Shall we leave it here, or one of us fly it?" Jim asked.

"Don't know that I'm so crazy about going in separate planes, Buddy, but they would surely think us nuts to leave one."

"That's what I was thinking. I'll pilot one and you take the other. We can mark this section on the chart and have a doctor or someone sent back to get Mills. He'll be all right for a few hours and it ought not to be hard to locate him, they can follow his trail of shells. He'll probably spill the whole lot as he goes."

"No sense in either of us trying to get him to civilization in one of the planes. If we leave him here, he might come out, just get enough sense to go up in it, then come down in a smash or run into some other machine."

"Yes. Let's get going."

Whistling and chuckling spasmodically the Flying Buddies set to work and presently they had the foliage screen out of the way, had wiped the sticky bodies of dead butterflies off the propellers and other parts, examined the control boards, the gas tanks, and then made a tryout test to be sure that everything was as it should be.

"Oh, gee, this is great. All set, Old Man?"

"Contact," Bob responded.

"Fore," bellowed Jim.

Presently they were in the cockpits, the engines roared merrily, it was great to hear them singing smoothly after the long silence and the Buddies waved at each other. The helicopter started first, ran a few rods, then lifted almost vertically and when it was off the ground, Bob's machine started taxiing swiftly, curved, its nose went up gracefully, then it began to climb, zooming swiftly until it reached the elevation Jim had attained. That done the boys smiled with satisfaction, circled about the spot in wide turns only climbing slightly. They took in the entire location, including the site of the ancient ruin, and after several minutes, Austin caught sight of Mills standing near the fallen stone. They saw the man stare up at them as if their presence in the sky puzzled him, then he bent over the ground and crouched out of sight, as if afraid.

Having ascertained his whereabouts, the two planes climbed again and when they were well in the ceiling, they leveled off, pointed their noses toward the sea, and with courses set, raced at high speed toward their goal. Mills' plane proved to be a faster machine than the Canadian Mountie's, but it gave a very good account of itself.

They had been flying nearly fifteen minutes when suddenly Jim spied a plane circling high in the distance. It banked, dipped, turned and came rushing toward them, the British insignia showing plainly on the fuselage. Soon it drew close and the Flying Buddies could see two men in her, one with a glass to his eyes, and in a moment the man waved; it seemed as if he were jumping up and down in the cock-pit, and the boys grinned widely as they realized that he was probably some airman who had spent long anxious hours in search of them. With a wave of his hand the pilot circled about them, then zoomed up, and shot forward at top speed toward the barracks airdrome.

"He's taking word in," Jim said to himself. It was wonderful to be going back to them, those kindly Britishers whose tongue and ideals were nearly like the Americans.

The little plane quickly outdistanced the boys and presently was only a speck on the horizon, but it seemed to Austin, even though the machine was swallowed up in the afternoon sunlight, there remained a bit of the nation's color in the heavens to signify that its fine men were ready to lend a hand, take a fair share of dangers, and understand. Jim felt as if it had been years since he and Bob had taken off from the smooth runway, watched the soldiers and people of the town wave after them, the cheers carrying on even above the roar of the machine. Since then the Flying Buddies had contacted with an entirely different sort of creature; it was rather like being dragged through miles of clinging, slimy mud, and what he wanted most of all at that moment was a good bath, but he didn't expect there was water enough in the world to rid them of the unwholesome association of Lang and his gang. Then he saw Bob pointing west of them and glanced in that direction. There were two other tiny specks which also zipped about and came rushing toward them swiftly as an arrow shot from a strong shaft. The boys slackened their own speed, and presently the two planes were racing along beside them, and then Bob guessed that the man at the controls was Bradshaw and his companion was Allen Ruhel. With a slight wave of the hand and a brief acknowledgement the three machines roared through the heavens. They were joined by one other plane, and an hour after leaving Mills at the ancient ruin, they were gliding down gracefully, while it looked to the boys as if everyone in the province had assembled to welcome them and learn what had happened. Soon the helicopter's wheels hit the ground, ran a short distance and stopped. Dozens of men came rushing to the side of the cockpit.

"Where have you been—"

"Are you hurt?"

"What happened to you?"

"Did you get blown off—"

"The whole country has been looking for you—"

"It's great that you are back safe—"

"Thank God you didn't have a smash-up." The queries and exclamations were hurled so fast it was impossible to answer, but in a moment, before Jim could loosen his strap, Allen Ruhel was beside him.

"Glad to see you, Old Top. Like to hop inside and freshen up a bit?" he asked casually as if the boys had not been gone more than a few hours.

"Like it better than anything else in the world," Jim answered, and Bradshaw looked at him narrowly.

"Anything we can do, just sing out—"

"I'd like to know about Mom," Bob announced a bit chokily, for he hoped hard that she had not been terrified by the news of the strange disappearance.

"Mrs. Austin is quite top hole, you know." Ruhel answered.

"She wasn't given all the particulars and a cable is off now to let them know that you came in under your own power," Bradshaw added. "The first man who sighted you sent it."

"Thanks a lot," Bob grinned. If his family was not suffering the agony of suspense, the rest did not matter, he thought.

"Come along," Captain Seaman invited.

It was a difficult task to get through the crowd which pressed about eagerly, and hundreds of hands, men's, women's and children's, touched those of the American boys who had come back. In the meantime they were safe, but they must be hungry and worn, although they did not look so bad—certainly not nearly so bad as if some airman had found them beneath the remains of a wrecked or burned machine. Thank God for that! Thank Him especially for the sake of their mother and father— after all, the world was pretty fine. Someone began to sing a medley of songs loved by Americans, and the Sky Buddies could hardly keep back the tears. It was wonderful having people who were so jolly to a fellow.

"Here are my quarters," Seaman smiled cordially. "You know them. Make yourselves at home—"

"Thanks a lot," Jim said chokily.

"Er, ah, the doctor is just across the way. By George, he's coming now. Decent sort of old sawbones. Let him give you the once over, it will perk him up no end, you know—"

"We're not hurt at all," Jim assured his host.

"To be sure, I didn't think you were, but you may as well be a good sport and give the old fellow something to do. Er, if you could dig a scratch, no matter how little, just enough to make him think you may be in danger of blood poisoning. We're such a bloody healthy bunch—I'll send him in, do what you can for him."

"All right," the boys agreed.

CHAPTER VIII
WHEN THE BUTTERFLIES DIE

After a good warm bath and a shower which helped the Buddies no end, they donned robes and admitted "Sawbones," a kindly old soldier whose real name was Manwell. He lost no time in preliminaries but in one swift, all-including glance, noted the ridges and welts left by the ropes that had bound the upper part of the strong young bodies for hours, the feet swollen from the long tramp, and the unmistakable dark rings under their eyes which evidenced lack of sleep.

"For a pair who are reported 'all right' you look a bit the worse for wear," he remarked gravely. "Stretch out on this cot and rest while I take your brother," he added to Jim.

"All right," Austin answered.

"We're not really brothers," Bob added. "Each of us started out with a whole pair of parents, but after Jim lost his mother and my father passed on, we looked each other over, decided that in union there is strength, so we got the two grown-ups married. Jim was his father's best man and I gave my mother away; that is I agreed to the arrangement as long as Jim's dad treated Mom all right, but it's understood I fill him full of lead if he falls down on the job." The doctor laughed heartily at this bit of family history.

"From all I have been able to gather Mr. Austin is still going around without any punctures," he chuckled.

"Yep, haven't even taken down a shot gun," answered Bob.

"Then you feel that you made no mistake," the doctor remarked.

"Sure," Jim put in. "I'd known Dad all my life; Bob knew his mother all his life, so we sort of guaranteed them to each other. Sometimes it doesn't work so good because my Dad's got the habit of acting perky because he's got two sons—"

"And Mom saves the gizzards for Jim and when there is only one piece of chocolate cake left, she cuts it three ways; I used to get it all." Bob scowled darkly.

"Looks as if trouble might be brewing," said Manwell.

"You still get the livers," Jim reminded his buddy.

"I like 'em better than the gizzards," said Bob calmly. He set his lips in a tight line when the doctor's fingers explored sore spots on his body, but although Manwell was highly efficient he was gentle and the lad realized it was better to submit to this thorough examination.

"Your disappearance yesterday caused a great deal of excitement," he remarked. "I understand that you were sighted above the Black Range. That's a pretty wild section, almost entirely unexplored; considered inaccessible. These marks were made by ropes, or some kind of thongs wound pretty tightly, but as far as I can see you have not suffered any serious injury; by that I mean you do not seem to have been hurt, struck or wounded. It will help me considerably if you will tell me something of your experience. There are uncivilized tribes far back among those hills. You must have been walked for hours—"

"We did walk for hours," Jim answered, "and we fell in with an uncivilized tribe of white men, not natives—"

"White men?"

"Yes. We were captured by a gang and made to do a Marathon; no Indian came near us, but we did see a few."

"Then I do not need to worry about the sort of treatment you might get from natives. I should have known it, for as long as the whites mind their own business, the natives attend very strictly to theirs." The doctor finished his examination of the younger boy, then turned his attention to Austin.

"We both got the same sort of deal," Jim explained.

"You'll be all right shortly, I'm sure, but I should like to keep an eye on you both for a few days," he told them, then went on chatting as he worked. "Did you happen to see the butterfly flight? I was up with a friend in the morning and saw a little of it."

"Reckon we saw it all—or a lot of it, anyway," said Jim.

"Pilots avoid them usually for they are apt to gum the works of the plane—"

"We were on the ground when it flew over so they did not force us down. It was a great sight, but sort of sad. I didn't know what it was at first, then I remembered reading that they do that every year;—it was thick as a cloud and when they got above us we couldn't see the sky."

"Marvelous sight, marvelous. Now you can slip into pajamas and soft slippers. Expect you'd like something to eat," the doctor smiled at them. "Naturally I'm keen to know what happened to you, but—"

"I say Doc, if we tell what happened to us no one will believe half of it, but I reckon I'd like to tell it to our friends from Canada and Captain Seaman, even if it does sound like—"

"Like a pack of fairy tales," added Bob.

"I say," there was a knock at the door and the voice was Ruhel's.

"Come on in, we were talking about you," Jim called, and the Canadian Mounty entered without further ceremony. "You're looking fit. If I had a horseshoe I'd pin it on you."

"Don't those boys want something to eat?" That was the Captain's wife, who was positive that her guests were famished.

"Expect they do," the doctor laughed, "although I cannot see that they have suffered especially from hunger."

"We didn't," Bob answered, but he did not say anything about the pellets they had eaten. Presently the Flying Buddies were seated in comfortable chairs before a dainty, but bountiful repast to which they did full justice. Captain Seaman, Ruhel, Bradshaw and the doctor were in the huge cool living room where the table was set, and although they were all agog to get the story of what had happened to the boys, they kept a discreet silence while the meal was in progress.

"Professor Martin to see you, Sir—" Before the servant could say anything more, a tall, thin, bespectacled man entered the room impatiently, and the British officer rose, and stared at him coldly.

"It is very important that I get in touch with you," the professor declared aggressively.

"Does it occur to you, Sir, that it might be equally important, possibly more so, that you remember your manners, if you have any, and that I should not be disturbed at this moment." His tones were cold as ice and the professor scowled.

"I am not usually considered lacking in manners, Captain," he retorted sharply.

"No?"

"No. It is important that I bring this matter to the authorities."

"The officer of the day will attend to whatever it is, Sir." The Captain bowed stiffly, an orderly literally backed the professor out of the room and the boys stared after him in astonishment.

"Does he own the earth?" Jim inquired.

"Or only an extra pair of socks?" added Bob.

"He's got a sore head," Seaman told them. "Came down among the islands with an important expedition as one of several scientists. They are doing a fine piece of work studying insect and vegetable life in the wild sections under a very capable man, chap named Morley, but he had to go home a few weeks ago because of illness and this lad Martin planted his feet in his chief's shoes, or has tried to. He's succeeded in making himself unpopular with the natives, not only those working for him but the villagers generally. A short time ago they did what you U. S.-er's call, 'walked out on him,' although they had been very satisfactory to Morley since he came nearly two years ago. Then Goodman tried to engage others, but didn't succeed. He is determined to carry the work in a section of the forests which they refuse to enter. He did manage in getting a few half-breeds and full bloods to go on the job, but they quit when the butterflies began to fly to the sea to die. It seems the insects, some of them, set their course above the workers, who are a superstitious lot. To them it is a sign of something, it is not clear to me just what it is."

"Does he have to conduct the investigation in that particular spot?" Jim inquired with interest.

"They say he does not. My own men, who know anything of the subject assure me that what they want to study and observe can be found in hundreds of localities. Morley and other men of the expedition were of the same opinion, they got along well with the native workers by keeping off their toes and being careful not to infringe with hobbies or ideas. Martin has been bull-headed in the matter and wants us to order the Indians to go out with him and do what he says. There is something about this Butterfly Flight; what is it Doc?"

"I don't know much more than you do except even if there isn't a butterfly in sight for miles, the natives seem to know when they are coming. They just knock off what they are doing and wait until it is over. Whatever signs they read from the flight governs their actions but as a rule the majority of them resume their jobs," he explained.

"We saw the flight," Bob remarked.

"Yes, one day of it. It takes several days. If Martin is sensible he'll take a week's vacation, for not even the negroes will help him now. He may as well turn his attention to something else for the present. How do you feel since you had something to eat?" The doctor asked.

"Top hole," declared Bob.

"Hadn't you both better have a good sleep now," Ruhel suggested.

"I'd like to tell you what we were doing before we go to bed. It may be hours before we wake up and in the meantime there's a white man back there—"

"A white man?" Seaman started to his feet.

"Yes, his name is Mills and he's gone crazy—"

"Crazy?" This exclamation came from the old doctor, then he turned gravely to the captain. "I do not want to be a butt-in, Seaman, but I should like to listen to this story, also, if the boys do not mind, I wish you would permit Donald to be present." He turned to Jim. "Donald is a full blooded native who has spent the greater part of his life with me and my wife. His mother died when he was an infant, she worked for us and we have brought the boy up. In deciding about his life we thought it best to keep him in touch with his own race so he spends a good part of his time with his native relatives. We have given him a Christian education, he is interested in things medical; and I do not mind telling you that he has given us a valuable education in many ways."

"I am sure Don will be interested in what you have to say, boys, and you can depend upon him to the last breath. He's a splendid fellow even if the doc did bring him up," the captain replied promptly.

"Surely, fetch him along," Jim agreed, then added, "But can we make the party sort of private! You are going to hear some whoppers and you'll know whether to send someone in after Mills. We didn't dare risk bringing him out."

"Very good." An orderly went in search of the doctor's adopted son and presently a tall young chap about seventeen years old, with fine manly bearing and a neat white suit but no hat, was ushered in. He was presented to the Flying Buddies, upon whom he smiled broadly, and then Morley explained why he had been sent for.

"I am honored," the young fellow nodded.

"Come along in my office," the captain invited, and soon the party were assembled about a huge table in an upper room. Orders were given that they were not to be disturbed on any account.

"Let's have a look at you," said the doctor. "Want to be sure your hearts and things are not going to be strained by lack of rest." He examined them quickly.

"All set?" Ruhel asked.

"You lead off, Jim," Bob said, so Jim started the story of their arrival on the clearing in the forest. He gave the exact location exactly as it showed on the plane's charts and indicators, and when the place was mentioned, Donald glanced at the doctor, then leaned forward lest he miss a word of the recital.

Austin told of the landing, seeing the ancient Indian who disappeared so mysteriously, their decision that one of them remain on guard and the boy drew a rough sketch of their location and position. Then Bob told them of his investigations, how much time he had spent, the sudden appearance of the javarel which split the sapling in front of him, then the three Indians, the coming of the butterflies, Jim's attempt to reach him and the arrival of the plane which had been forced down by the cloud of insects.

"Those white butterflies flew over your head?" Donald interrupted.

"Not while I stood there, but when I stepped out of course I got into them," Bob replied.

"May I ask another question. Where did you get those rings you are wearing?" the Indian boy wanted to know. Jim eyed him narrowly for a moment.

"They were given to us by a boy in Vermont some time ago. It was during the floods and we carried him and his uncle across Lake Champlain so they could take the train in New York," he replied carefully. He had a hunch that Donald knew something about the rings.

"We didn't do much, but everyone was having a bad time, so they gave us the rings because they appreciated getting away," Bob added.

"Thank you," Donald smiled. "Pardon the interruption," he turned to the captain. "I've seen similar rings and could not resist inquiring."

"That's all right, old man," Seaman replied.

"The second plane landed near us," Jim went on with the story, but he omitted the argument over the green emeralds because he did not wish to bring in Don Haurea if he could help it, although both Ruhel and Bradshaw had met the scientist when they were in Texas looking for young Gordon.

"If I may interrupt, I should like to ask Donald what difference it made whether the butterflies went over the boys' heads," Ruhel said. "The doctor spoke of superstitions regarding the annual flight." The dark boy smiled.

"It is said that one who deliberately runs into or under them in their flight will meet disaster in a short time, and all with him," he replied.

"I see, thank you."

"Our Flying Buddies did not deliberately run into them," Bradshaw said gravely.

"They did not, Sir."

"Great guns, Goodman, the professor I mean, did run into them deliberately—" Seaman put in soberly.

"He did and he endeavored to take workers with him. That is why they deserted him," Donald explained.

"I see. Manwell would have investigated and avoided such an act," the Captain remarked, then went on, "Excuse me, boys. Please proceed with your story."

"Yes sir." Jim took it up, told of entering the forest with their arms bound, the long wearisome tramp, the destruction of Red, the loss of the batteries and food. The boy told the tale as simply as possible, and although none of the audience asked another question, there were numerous exclamations of astonishment, and several times one of the men paced up and down the floor as the facts were revealed. At last they came to the brightening of the tunnel, the change of air and finally the appearance of the Indian band with their treasures. "When the last of them passed he stopped and looked at Mills for a moment, then went on."

"Stopped and looked at Mills?" said the doctor.

"Yes sir." The old man looked at his young adopted son, who nodded his head gravely.

"The man you said that you left back there?"

"Yes. He's crazy as a bed-bug—"

"Please proceed," Donald urged.

"Well," Jim glanced around. "I don't begin to understand this part at all and I shall not blame you if you set it down as a pipe dream." He turned to Bob. "We haven't discussed it between ourselves, Buddy, so you listen carefully and check up on what I tell them. Chip in if I'm wrong anywhere."

"Shoot," Bob replied, so Austin proceeded with the tale of the appearance of the band, through the final destruction of both white men and dark, by the released waters.

"I say, Don," the doctor's voice was low and not very steady, "is that Bloody Dam—the place where—"

"I believe so, Sir." He turned to Bob. "You were beside your step-brother, would you please tell us this part of the story as you saw it?"

"It's about the same as Jim. I had a feeling that it was a dream, but the whole thing seemed sort of unreal and I didn't think of the Indian band as different from everything else, not until I came out and was where I could pay any attention to the things separately," Bob replied, then he went on telling how he had crouched by the tree, cautiously wriggling until he got his teeth in the rope to chew it apart. Jim's appearance just before the task was finished and cutting the lariat with his knife. He proceeded with the account of the Indians, the final swirling of the water almost to their feet and its receding as it found the lower outlet. When the boy paused, his face was white and drawn.

"Suppose you have a drink of this," the doctor urged. He stirred something, in a glass of water, gave some to each of the lads, and in a moment their tenseness relaxed somewhat and the color came back to their faces.

"Thank you," said Jim, then started with the rest of the narrative.

CHAPTER IX
THE GHOSTS OF BLOODY DAM

There were no further interruptions during the unfoldment of the crowded hours of the Flying Buddies until the final flight for the British barracks. There was a general sigh of relief and a smile when the men listened to that part in which the lads had discovered that they had made a circle in their wanderings and had returned to their starting point. Numerous pipes had been lighted and permitted to go out during the recital, and when Jim finished, Captain Seaman struck his tenth match and puffed vigorously. Only the doctor and his adopted son did not soothe tensed nerves with the narcotic. The room was as still as if it were empty when the boy's voice ceased, but finally Bradshaw broke the silence.

"There would have been a howl which could have been heard from Chili to Quebec if some of the pilots had discovered you lost within a few yards of the plane," he grinned.

"Surely would," Jim admitted.

"Will you send to search for Mills?" Bob asked their host, but before the captain could answer, Donald spoke.

"It will be as well, if I may be allowed to express an opinion, to let him remain as he is for the present."

"Until the last butterfly passes?" asked the doctor.

"Yes sir, until the last butterfly passes," the lad replied.

"He might injure himself or starve," Seaman objected, but he made no move to start the search.

"He will not starve, for the forest is full of berries, larger fruits and roots upon which he will learn to sustain himself. He found a fire lighted and will probably have sense enough to keep it going. Even if he doesn't, he need not suffer. The ruin has many nooks in which he can protect himself from cold or storms if it is necessary—"

"But snakes, or wild animals—" Bob protested.

"They will not molest him," Donald insisted.

"If we send air men in after him are they likely to be in danger?" Seaman asked quietly.

"They are." He turned to the Flying Buddies. "I believe that you are the first white men who have been through the Black Range Woods, seen what you have seen, and lived to tell your story," he told them quietly.

"I've heard that no white man who entered them during the time of the Butterfly Flight ever came out. As a matter of fact, I understand they have never been heard from again," the doctor added soberly.

"We were lucky," Jim answered.

"I say," Bob turned to the young Indian. "Tell us about this thing, will you?" He glanced about the room. "I'm sure we should all be glad to hear something and none of us will speak of it outside this room."

"You can depend upon us," Ruhel spoke up.

"Well—" Donald glanced at his father.

"Donald doesn't often discuss the—er things which are very close to his people," Manwell answered for the boy. "Not even with us."

"There are some things I may tell you," he replied, "but they must not be repeated before the womenfolk. I shall be glad to have this opportunity to talk of them now if we will not be interrupted." He glanced at the captain. Immediately that gentleman went to the door, and signaled to an orderly who stood at attention further down the hall.

"I shall be occupied here for a time. Is anyone in the house?"

"No sir. Madam has gone to the garden party, and the servants are in their own quarters, sir."

"Excellent. Have a couple of the boys keep watch outside so that no one comes near."

"Yes sir."

"Thank you."

He closed the door and a moment later they heard the click of heels as the guard hurried to see that the command was carried out explicitly. In the meantime the men puffed, the doctor glanced a bit anxiously at his patients, while the young Indian sat as still as if he had been carved out of some fine dark marble. Jim's eyes traveled over the well-shaped head, and thought of Ynilea, their special friend in the great Laboratory, and he wondered if this young fellow might not be receiving some of his training in one of the marvelous underground schools. He recalled that Don Haurea had told him that the world was ready for some of the information those scientific men had proved and it was possible that this lad, because of his advantages as a doctor's son might have been chosen to bring out for humanity medical or surgical truths still unknown to modern life. He remembered too, that the doctor had said that Donald had "been an education" to himself and his wife. Perhaps the story the lad would tell them would answer the questions Austin dared not ask at this time. He rather hoped they would get an opportunity to be alone with Donald before the "Lark" was ready to take them north again.

"It seems to me you boys are making a rather long day of it," said Bradshaw with a scowl.

"Why remind us of that? This looks like the best time in the world, and if we know a little of the truth of the Black Woods and the Dam, we can go to sleep in peace and not spend hours tossing around while our feeble brains try to find a solution—"

"Feeble is good," said Bradshaw with a grin. Just then they heard the two guards pacing back and forth and the orderly returned to his station in the hall.

"Guess it's all set," the captain told them.

"You know," Donald looked at their host, "that Doctor Manwell adopted me when my mother died. I was a baby and he and his wife have been most—"

"Why not skip that part?" the doctor put in quickly.

"I shall try not to embarrass you, sir, but I may as well mention the fact so everyone will understand," he said, then went on, "They have brought me up as carefully as if I were their own son, taught me themselves, hired tutors, and sent me to good schools—"

"That you ran away from, you young rascal," the doctor chuckled.

"You had already taught me all they could and I wanted to be with you, work with you," he replied. "As long as I can remember some of my own race have been near me. It has always been my privilege to visit them and they too have instructed me. I am especially interested in my father's profession and with his help hope to carry it on—I hope I can become as honored as he is—"

"My boy, my boy—"

"Please don't interrupt. That's not cricket," said Bob.

"Pardon me."

"Because of this desire in me, my own people have taught me the numerous herbs which grow hereabouts, the chemicals that can be extracted from them, the trees, soil, and even insects. I have not learned a great deal as yet—"

"I may as well throw in a bouquet myself. Everything he has shown to me is new to medical science, and has proved of great value in curing illnesses considered incurable," the doctor told them.

"Thank you, sir. As well as these matters, I have learned much about my own race, its traditions, history before the conquest and the destruction of the Empire. All of these things are fairly well known to you, so I shall go to the story of the temple ruin the boys visited earlier this morning. It was an ancient city long before the Spaniards visited these shores, had a large population, while many of its leading men knew of the Ynca Empire to the south. The tribes frequently traded with each other, and it was the ambition of our race to extend the northern section of the development to meet that of the Yncas which ended, at the time of the conquest, at Quito, which was the last great station on the Royal Road," he paused, and Jim nodded.

"We've seen some of the ruins," Jim said.

"No doubt, the land is full of them. In the temple were men and women, the best of the tribes, who recorded the traditions and history in sculpturing, carving, weaving and the knotted twines which are still found in certain localities. The range of the Andes mountains which separated us from the southern empires was, and still is, a great barrier. There were no horses, wagons or other means of building, but construction was going on constantly. Then our ancient prophets who foretold many things with great accuracy, and read the signs in the skies, the rocks, and the mountains, grew very sober. They foretold that the Empire to the south would be annihilated almost entirely and a new race would take complete possession of the whole country."

"Those prophets surely knew their onions," Bob remarked, and Donald nodded.

"They met with the great men of the land, and for the next hundred years they ceased to build in the sections of the Black Woods. They devoted themselves to planting great forests, to cutting ways through the mountains which are still undiscovered by the white men, and quietly started a community far from the coast, and so distant from other tribes that their existence in the new community was unknown. Each new generation studied the signs, and although many of the people were discontented because of the activities carried on, which were in opposition to their own desires, the younger prophets continued to verify the findings of the old men, so that no change was made in the plan. The people who did not believe that it was possible for a strange race to come here and survive, separated themselves from the others and resolved to remain where they were. However, they did assist in the construction of hiding-houses and passages to which they could flee if the threatened danger ever came. The southern empire was growing both north and south and our people, some of them, were sure the others lacked what you now call a progressive spirit." He smiled at the Flying Buddies.

"Great old spirit," Bob remarked.

"Over a hundred years from the time of the first prophecy, tribes coming from the northern islands began to tell strange tales of a race which came out of the sea in winged boats, spit fire from sticks, and threw red hot stones which caused everything they struck to crumble and fall. They dressed in a shiny metal and mounted themselves on strange animals they called horses, whose hoofs trampled men, women and children. They spoke of their king, made amazing promises to the natives, stole gold and jewels by the boat-load, and forced the tribes to work for them and pay them tribute."

"Generous little habit those middle-agers had," said Jim.

"The people of our land heard these stories and most of them withdrew to the fastness they had prepared for themselves, but the others refused to credit the strange stories and could not conceive of any race making slaves of them. They built themselves more hiding places, buried their treasures, made circuitous passages through the thick forests and filled them with spiked traps, deadly snakes, vipers, and treacherous bridges which would fall as soon as any weight was put upon them. They deserted their city and temple, and stripped it of its wealth. In the course of a few years the white men appeared in their boats, threw their hot stones, or bullets, fired their guns, and marched into the land. They found, here in the north, a few wild tribes besides all that was left of our people who had remained behind."

"Reckon they wished they had gone when the going was good," said Jim.

"One day they learned that a new army of white men was coming, so a band carrying the treasures of the temple with them started by a roundabout route to join the distant community. They marched through their passage to a deep meadow where they expected to find an opening by which they could continue their journey, but they discovered that a solid wall rose in front of them and that behind it a stream had formed a good-sized lake. Some of the men went to locate a route around this. While the others waited, the white men appeared with their guns, armor, horses and blood thirsty dogs. They destroyed the band, took the treasure, and being unfamiliar with the country, started their horses up the cliffs, which were rugged and appeared possible to ascend. In the struggle and the scrambling, stones were loosened, a stream burst through and the entire wall gave way, killing them all."

"But that was hundreds of years ago," protested Jim.

"Yes, over four hundred," Donald replied. "The men of the band who went in search of a passage met a party of hunters from the new community. Their prophets had foreseen the disaster and these men were on their way to help their people if they could. When they reached the spot they saw the destruction which had been wrought and grieved deeply, for among the dead were many of their own relatives."

"Pretty tough," said Bob.

"One of the old prophets from the temple was with the party. They spent three days at the lake, fasting and praying to the sun, then they cursed the site, the Black Woods, all that was in it, and all that came into it. As they prayed the heavens grew dark, although it was day; a great comet shot across the sky, leaving a long pathway of green light which did not fade for many hours. By this sign the men knew that their prayers were answered. They cursed the place again, willed that the spirits of their slaughtered companions should return every year through all time as long as the white butterflies passed over the land to the sea; that the white men who had destroyed the band should repeat their crime and again take their punishment as meted out to them by the stored-up waters of the lake."

"Whew," exploded Bradshaw and he mopped his forehead.

"They further willed that any man who deliberately forced himself into the woods and under the butterflies should find destruction before the moon changed," the boy went on solemnly. "That while the spirits of those men of the temple walked the earth, if one of them gazed on a white man, met his eyes, that man should go mad, should live the life of an animal, so that no animal should injure him, but he should burrow in the ground for shelter as long as he lived, and that he should thus pass a span of years equal to the life time of three men—"

"Good God," whispered Ruhel.

"They surely made a good job of it while they were at it," Jim said softly.

"The last we saw of Mills, he was digging in," added Bob, and there was no mirth in his tone.

"And he's got three life-times to serve," said the doctor sadly, then added, "I have seen two men in the forests who seemed to be doing the same thing—they are so old no one knows how many years they have lived."

"That is why I said we must leave Mills. He would fight you like a demon, probably injure your men who tried to help him—"

"He picked up that chap who was with the dwarf and tossed him about as if he were a rubber ball," Bob reminded them.

"The strength of a man who is insane," said Ruhel. "We've had some dealings with them in Canada, powerful woodsmen, and it takes almost the whole force to overcome one."

"Guess we've all had such experiences," said Seaman. He smoked thoughtfully and stared at Donald.

"Now you know the story of the Bloody Dam. There are few of the natives who really know the tale, but every year someone brings out evidence that the Black Woods must be avoided; many legends have grown up about it, and neither the natives nor the negroes will go into it at this time of the year. You are in charge of this section of the country, Captain Seaman, my father and mother have made their home here, so I received permission to tell you the story that you might understand," he finished impressively.

"Thanks no end. It will probably save us many difficulties," the captain answered, and he gave no sign of doubting the strange tale. "I've been in these parts many years and I've seen queer things—"

"Jinks, isn't there any end to the curse?" Bob demanded. "Surely those old fellows ought to be satisfied with four hundred years of punishment."

"And their own people have to be a part of it," Jim added.

"As long as the butterflies make their flight to the sea," Donald replied. "The Black Woods and range are really a small area of land, probably about fifty miles square, and all white men will do well to keep out of it."

"It's a small space to avoid, considering the extent of the land where one can travel with safety," said Seaman. "It happened to be on the edge of my province and I'm willing to give it a wide berth, but it does seem as if there must be some way of cleaning it up."

"Better concentrate on cleaning up things nearer at hand," the doctor advised, then he turned to the Buddies. "In spite of my son's story I can see that your lids are heavy. You must not make your bodies pay too dearly because of your adventure. Get into a couple of bunks and forget the world for the next few hours."

"Reckon you are right," Jim replied, and he did have difficulty suppressing a yawn.

"We shall not need rocking," Bob added, then he held out his hand to Donald. "Thanks a lot for telling us what it was all about. We have to hang around here for a few days until our plane is in ship shape again. She bumped her nose on an iceberg, or something like that, and has to have her face lifted. Hope we see you again before we leave."

"My hope is the same. Rest as my father advises and when you have waked perhaps the Captain will send up an American flag to let us know that all is well with you—"

"Nothing of the kind," the captain declared. "But I'll have the boys run our own flag up and down so you'll get the word quickly."

CHAPTER X
AN INVITATION

It was not yet sundown when the Sky Buddies finally got to bed, and as Bob said, they did not need to be rocked; they went to sleep almost as soon as their weary heads touched the pillows. Long after breakfast had been served in the Captain's home the next morning they opened their eyes at about the same minute. Shades had been drawn to darken the rooms but through a crack Jim could see light, so his first thought was that he had probably rested about an hour, but Bob had a view of the clock which contradicted such an idea.

"Wow," he exclaimed, seeing that his step-brother was awake, "it's tomorrow, Old Timer."

"G'wan," Jim growled. "I've hardly been asleep."

"Go back if you want to, but I'm hollow to my boots—"

"Then hustle up and the trouble shall be immediately corrected." That was Mrs. Seaman who had been listening for a sign that her guests might soon begin to feel as if they had caught up with the sandman.

"Is that a threat or a promise?"

"Both. Good morning. My husband looked in on you a couple of times before he went on duty, and said to let you have it out," she smiled. "I'll have the orderly run the water for your baths and you can take things easy today. Those are orders," she told them.

"And we always obey orders," Jim answered. Now that he knew it was late, he banished the idea of another doze, stretched, yawned, and would have thrown a pillow at Bob if they had been at home, but guests in a stranger's house have to be more circumspect. Their toilet did not take very long, for in the warm climate few clothes are required, and presently the pair, feeling fit as a couple of fiddles, presented themselves to their hostess, who looked them over with frank approval.

"You appear to be top hole," she said.

"And we are," Jim assured her.

While they were at breakfast one of the men came in with word that the boat was leaving for the "bug settlement" to take Doctor Manwell on his weekly inspection of the workers. Donald was making the trip with his adopted father, and if the Flying Buddies cared to accompany the expedition, there was plenty of room and they were quite welcome.

"That's the place Martin is managing, isn't it?" Jim asked.

"Yes. They were having some difficulties yesterday, but I expect it is over by now. Those disagreements come up and pass quickly. I have also been invited, and I have been delighted to accept. Mrs. Manwell and a couple of other women are also going along. We'll have rather a jolly time."

"Sounds mighty interesting to me," Bob told her.

"Then it is settled that we go. Donald will come and let us know when they are ready to start," Mrs. Seaman explained.

Half an hour later the Indian lad, neat as a pin in his fresh white suit, arrived to escort the party to the launch. They drove from the barracks, out though the little white town with its conglomeration of ancient and modern dwellings and small stores, along the shore road where they had a wonderful view of the water, blue as a sapphire, and finally stopped on the wharf where the doctor, his wife and the rest of the party had already assembled. Mrs. Manwell was a kindly looking woman, somewhat younger than her husband, and she presented two young friends, Phyllis and Barbara Harding and their mother.

"We have been planning to take the trip to the 'bug settlement' for some time," Mrs. Harding told the Flying Buddies with a cordial smile, "but we residents of the islands are the greatest procrastinators in the world; it is only when we have guests with us that we exert ourself to show off our country."

"Bob is a bug-nut; crazy about insect and plant life, so he'll have a whale of a time," Jim told her. "I enjoy seeing what people are studying, but I haven't got as much brains for it as Buddy."

"We'll have a picnic lunch and you can see Dr. Manwell's clinic. He takes care of both the natives and whites, babies and all," said Phyllis, who was a jolly sort of girl.

"It'll be great," Bob declared enthusiastically.

"I suppose you would prefer traveling by plane," Mrs. Manwell said.

"It's quicker, but we like to be on the earth sometimes and have a good look at her. Look at those fishes!" A whole school went scooting past, some of them darting out of the water as if they too were thoroughly enjoying themselves.

The boat made its way about a quarter of a mile from the coast, its nose plowing a deep trough and its stern leaving a wide triangular trail of rollers and foam. There was just enough breeze to make the trip delightful and the picnickers jollied each other at a lively rate as they sped along. It took nearly an hour to reach the mouth of the small river they expected to go up, and when they finally turned inland the change from the vast expanse to the narrower waterway, with its swamps, extravagant growths and forests, made the Flying Buddies exclaim with wonder.

"Wouldn't you prefer to be flying?" Barbara asked.

"This is immense," Bob told her. "I suppose the men of the expedition have an airplane."

"They have two," the engineer answered, "but only one is at camp now. It's a triple motor with a cabin, but the pilot has been sick for a couple of days so it has been out of use. The other chap flew to Jamaica to get some special equipment and will not be back for a couple of days."

"My father is to see from what the pilot is suffering," Donald remarked. "He did not let anyone know he did not feel well until this morning."

"I hope it is not anything serious, poor fellow. He should have been brought in to town, it seems to me."

"We wanted him to come, but he insisted he'd do all right if the doctor came and looked him over," said the engineer.

"If he would be better in town, we will fetch him back," Dr. Manwell announced confidently.

They were making their way through a swift pass between high, overhanging cliffs, and ten miles further along they saw the outskirts of the tiny settlement with its rows of tents, log cabins, community houses, and native's quarters. There seemed to be very few persons about, but a couple of white boys came to meet the boat when it reached the dock, and caught the hawser the engineer tossed to them.

"I suppose you want to go right to the village, sir, but I thought our young American friends would like to go around the loop and get a good look at the works, whatever is near here," the engineer said, and he glanced at the Buddies.

"That's an excellent idea. It will not take long. I shall visit my patients, and suggest that the ladies of the party get things ready for our picnic luncheon," the doctor proposed.

"We will do that, and some of us may be able to help you," Barbara spoke up quickly, because she had made up her mind that when she was old enough she was going to be a nurse. The plan was adopted, and as the landing party was helped ashore, the two southern boys eyed the Flying Buddies with interest.

"Where is Professor Martin?" the Doctor inquired.

"He went off with a party of natives early this morning. They have been angry with him, so I guess he's trying to square himself by giving them a feast and a holiday," the older lad replied.

"That's good. He'll find that he will make much better progress if he is a little patient in his dealings with them," said the doctor. "I suppose that is why you two lads are alone."

"I don't like the Prof. and don't care about his parties, but the native children and their mothers, most of them, went along with the men. I guess they are going to hunt and have a great time, but I'd rather stay when you are due," the younger lad answered frankly, and the doctor smiled.

"All ashore who are going ashore?" the engineer called. "Got the luggage?"

"Everything and everybody," laughed Phyllis.

"Then we're off." The hawser was drawn in, looped about its own hook, the engine started again, and the launch went chug-chug-chugging back into the middle of the stream, the party on shore waved, and the Buddies waved back.

"Its great of you to think of taking us around," said Bob.

"It occurred to me that you would get a better view of things, a more general one, if we went around the loop. By that I mean up a branch of the river and across into where the main stream turns. This water does more twisting around than you can shake a stick at, and when we first came down we had to do a lot of exploring before we knew that it was all one stream, not half a dozen. The pilots helped with that job. Any other way would have taken weeks, for the forest is so thick in most places that a man has to chop his way through. The site of our principal investigations is an island, really, and the bug-men seem to have found more specimens than they ever realized existed. I didn't think much of the job when I got it, but I'm as interested as all the rest in what they have accomplished," Howard went on pleasantly, and both boys thought he was splendid.

"We heard that it came here under another leader," Jim remarked.

"It did, and believe me, it won't be long before the present incumbent gets his walking papers. That's one thing the pilot is going to engineer in Jamaica, because Martin is a bad man. He thinks he knows everything, won't listen to anyone, and has caused more trouble in a few weeks than we've had in the two years we've been here," he told them.

"Too bad he's such a die-hard," said Jim.

"Now, here we are. Look ahead there, I'll go a bit slow. See that scaffolding way up high?" He pointed to the right and the boys saw the framework above a thick roof of foliage, and even as they watched, could see a couple of men moving slowly along it and apparently examining something with magnifying glasses.

"Are they getting specimens?" Jim asked.

"Yes. They have discovered that insect life exists in layers. The bugs that live above that foliage screen are different from those below it, and in a place as high as that, there are sometimes several species in the woods underneath."

"Expect they get some wonderful butterflies," said Bob, who had a fine collection of his own at home.

"Indeed they do. You can see them before you go. They have dozens of cases, and have already sent crates of them to the museums all over the world." They passed this first station, and then putting on more speed went rushing swiftly over the water, which was dark green and very deep. The boys were intensely interested in this part of the trip, and when the men in the stations noticed the boat, they shouted to Howard and waved greetings to the visitors.

"Do they mind being away off alone?" Jim asked.

"Reckon they get homesick sometimes, but there are radios, and that sort of thing in camp, and when the job is finished they will each get a good vacation to make up for such a lot of hard work. Here we can go ashore." Howard ran the boat close to the land, made it fast to a sapling, and then led the way to where several men were busy collecting, assorting and classifying the lower strata of insect life. They all nodded a cheery greeting to the guests, showed them some of the exhibits, and the paraphernalia, and Bob was so interested that he wished he could spend a month with those busy fellows.

"You will get a chance to read about what we have accomplished and that will be easier than staying here," one chap laughed.

"Gosh, a fellow would like to live half a dozen lives to take in all the good things that are going on," said Bob.

"Great age we're living in, but even a bug can teach us no end."

"We are going all the way around, so we'd better start," Howard reminded them, so with a sigh, Caldwell tore himself away, and presently the three were back in the launch, chugging off from the shore and its interesting workers. They made two more stops before they reached the branch stream, where the researchers were all stationed on high scaffolds.

"Their stuff went to camp yesterday, so you wouldn't see anything different," Howard told them and they chugged by. The branch was so narrow and winding that it took all his skill to pilot his boat, and the boys were thrilled with the wonders all about them.

There were hundreds of great vines, heavy with fruit and flowers, enormous interlocking trees through which birds of brilliant plumage flashed swift as streaks. Some of them called hoarsely to the boatmen, while others, far back, paused in their flight to trill their own sweet melodies. Hundreds of monkeys of all sizes chattered at them or swung from branches with inquisitive glances, and twice, impudent rascals threw pieces of wood defiantly after them. They saw a couple of little fellows leaping along the shore evidently curious about the great rollers the boat left behind it, but when one extra large wave swept over the leader, he leaped to the nearest tree and scolded roundly.

"You were looking for it," Bob chuckled.

"Like to take one home?" Howard asked. "The boys have caught a few, but they usually let them go."

"I'd rather leave them here where they belong," Bob answered. "I do not believe they would take to an airplane."

"Oh, you don't? That's where you are wrong. The pilot who went to Jamaica found one stowed away in his bus when he first came down, and he's been with him ever since. The little pest won't leave the machine as long as he has his aviation suit on."

"Tell us another."

"That one is true. When they get up where it's cold, he gets into the chap's pocket and pulls down the flap. That's a fact. There was a story about it in the papers and a picture of the pair of them in the plane," Howard insisted.

"Reckon we'll have to believe it." Jim eyed a small monkey who was clinging, frightened to his mother. "If it wasn't for your parents, I'd take you along," he called, and as if the mother understood, she ran along the branches until she was ahead of the boat, then stopped and scolded furiously. "It's all right, you needn't get so het up about it—I haven't taken him."

"He's admiring him, you flapper," Bob shouted. "You should be flattered instead of mad."

"Now we're on the last stretch," Howard announced as the boat turned again. "It's five miles by water to the village; three by airline."

"It was great of you to take us around," said Jim.

"Surely was," added Bob.

"Glad you liked it. We don't usually take parties over the route because they are not always careful, but I had what you American boys call a hunch that you would appreciate it and not do any damage. The site of the work isn't generally known because the professors did not want to be pestered with too many visitors, but a few have come. Some of the scientific publications have sent writers to get articles, but several of the men working here send out that sort of stuff themselves, so only special men have been taken around the works," Howard explained.

"Sounds as if we are nearing the village," Jim remarked a bit later, because he heard voices quite distinctly.

"We are near, and not near. We couldn't get across here, but it's only about a quarter of a mile if we could go through. It's a mile and a half by the boat."

"Suppose they did not want to cut the place up too much."

"No. They have had to do a lot of that anyway," Howard answered. They were going through what appeared like a natural passage over which the great branches formed an arch, and through the openings, the boys caught glimpses of numerous parrots, some plain green, almost the shade of the trees in which they perched, while others were gaily colored with bright red and yellow, their long tails hanging gorgeous and graceful.

"I should not mind having one of them to take home to Mom," Bob remarked, "but she'd be displeased if I caught it and brought it away to live the rest of its life in a cage. My mother doesn't like to see things confined."

"On the Cross-Bar ranch all the pens and corrals have to be huge. Even the pigs have spacious quarters; so big they won't fatten. The foreman built a small one where she doesn't notice it," Jim added with a grin.

"Doesn't she miss them?" Howard asked.

"He's managed so far to see that she doesn't," Bob replied, "but he's lucky that she keeps away from the pigs pretty much."

"I see—"

"O—o—" Just then a shrill scream came so clearly and sounded so startling that the Flying Buddies sprang to their feet. "O—"

"Is something the matter?" Jim asked quietly.

"That sounds like a woman's scream," Bob added, and their faces paled as the panic-stricken cry came again.

"It is a woman," Howard answered, and he opened up his engine, putting on every ounce of power he dared, and bending low as the boat shot along the treacherous waterway.

CHAPTER XI
REVENGE! REVENGE!

"Have you got any guns aboard?" Jim asked tensely.

"No. There are a good many in the settlement and at the stations, but I've never bothered to carry any on the boat," Howard answered.

Then again came the frightened cry of a woman, followed by a number of screams, which stopped suddenly as if a hand had been placed over the mouth that uttered them. With straining eyes the Buddies tried to peer through the tall, impenetrable foliage which grew on both sides of them, while the engineer stared tensely ahead lest he send his boat on the rocks that lined the way. It seemed to them as if hours passed, although it was only a few minutes before they raced around the last turn and shot forward into a wider stretch of water at the further end of the village.

At first they could not see anything unusual about the community, but as they went along they made out a confused collection of native men and women. The white people among them appeared to be herded in the middle, and the moment the engine was silenced, startled voices cried protestingly, as the huge Indians crowded close. Jim heard one voice above the others, speaking a language he did not know, and recognized Don's clear tones which sounded cool and determined. Howard brought the boat up to the beach, but he hesitated a moment.

"Thinking of taking some of them off?" Bob whispered and the man nodded his head.

"Looks as if the natives have jumped on the whites for some reason or other," he answered. "I don't want to hop out if we can get the women away, but those fellows look ugly and our chances are mighty slim, I'm afraid."

"Wait here for us," Jim said softly. Then he leaped ashore, his hands dug deep in his coat pockets, and Bob, not knowing what was in his step-brother's mind, followed suit.

"Better keep on the outer edge of them," Howard warned.

"We will!" Jim ran a few yards, and yelled at the top of his lungs. "You fellows want a bomb or two right in the middle of you?" He drew one fist up as if it held something large and deadly, and a few of the men faced him quickly, but the others merely crowded closer to the white women and sneered defiantly.

"No kill own women," one declared.

"Don't kid yourself," Jim reported quickly. "I'll blow up the lot of you in about a half a minute." He looked exactly as if he meant every word of it, and he did, but there was nothing more dangerous in his pocket than a small flashlight. Then he saw Donald standing close beside his mother and father, whose arms were bound with thongs. "What's it all about?" he demanded. The young Indian spoke to the men nearest him; presently there was a silence, and he faced Jim.

"I am glad that you appeared with your bombs, Mr. Austin, you and your brother, but I pray that you will not use them immediately. I am sure the men here will listen to reason," he said elaborately.

"They won't have much time to listen to reason. Where I come from we make a practice to shoot or throw our bombs first and apologize afterwards," Jim snapped, and his eyes blazed furiously. "I heard those women scream. Tell those fellows to take their hands off, or I won't listen to anything— not a thing!"

"I will," Donald said quickly. Both boys knew that a good many of the natives understood perfectly what was said, and now those who were nearest to the belligerent-looking young Texans stepped away from their captives. Donald interpreted the speech, and the other women were promptly released.

"That's better. Now, what's the trouble," Jim thundered, and was glad that his voice was a deep one.

"Professor Martin took a party of men, women and children into the woods. They thought they were going to have a party and a feast but he lead them to the Black Woods, into which they will not go until after the last butterfly has passed over to the sea."

"Yes," Jim snapped.

"He guided them into a passage he had found which lead them through the thickest part of the forest. Some of the men got suspicious and asked questions, then they all refused to go on, but the professor had herded the women and children ahead of him along with a couple of huge brutes he'd picked up in town. They forced the women to go on, and threatened to shoot the men if, they did not come with him and work where he wished."

"I see."

"They went along and were coming up a grade, when they heard strange sounds, the tramping of many feet. They broke and ran back."

"Well."

"They could not bring the women and children with them, so to be revenged, they came back and determined to kill every white woman and man they found here."

"Yes." Jim was thinking hard and he certainly wished that his pockets were full of explosives.

"They gathered up friendly tribes to help them, and landed here about half an hour ago, took possession of all the guns in the settlement, drove the native women away, and captured the white women," Donald explained.

"Don't they know the professor will come back with their families?" Bob asked.

"At this time none may come back from the Black Woods," one man declared sullenly. "None comes out alive."

"The Professor, who is a fool, will himself never come back. He took children, our children, to their deaths," another put in darkly.

"For the loss of them, we take the white women," snapped a third, and his hand went toward Phyllis' shoulder.

"Hold off," Jim snapped, stepping forward quickly, and the hand remained suspended in the air. "Now, listen to me, you fellows, I'll get your women and children out of the Black Forest, or Woods—"

"They will be dead—none comes out alive—never since the curse of Bloody Dam."

"Let me tell you something, you men. I was in the Black Woods, I've been at the Bloody Dam, my buddy here and I were there the first day the butterflies started their flight, and we came out alive—"

"You lie—"

"I do not lie. We heard the baying of the dogs, saw the fall of the stone wall, the wall on which the ancient prophet stood when he cursed all who entered the Black Woods—"

"You saw and heard?" An old man came close. "Did one of them look into your eyes?" The voice shook and the man's lips trembled.

"None looked into my eyes, nor my buddy's eyes," Jim answered solemnly, "and we came through, past poison snakes, over rotten logs, and now, on the ancient ruin there is a white man into whose eyes the last man of the band gazed. The man is mad, he was digging a hole in the ground when we saw him last."

"This is true," Donald added; then he spoke in their own tongue and the natives stared at the two white boys as if they were beings from some other world.

"How can you bring our children back?" one asked and his lips were set in a firm line.

"There is an airplane here. We will go to fetch them. Howard, who is in the boat, where there are more bombs, will stand guard. You must let the white women go to the shore and no man must lay a hand on them until we return. Do you understand?"

"You will go to the settlement for soldiers," one snarled.

"I will go to the Black Woods, to the Bloody Dam if need be, for your children, and I will fetch them back. I do not lie," he declared with great soberness.

"You shall go. The white woman may assemble near the boat with the engineer; but if in three-quarters of an hour you have not returned, they shall all be destroyed," the old man answered, and the other nodded their assent.

"You have been in the Black Woods and you cannot lie," a younger man spoke sharply. "If we do not hear the loud purr of your engines in the time set, they shall die. While you are gone, many of the friendly tribe will post themselves so that they will know if you do not keep your word, and if but one soldier appears, all shall be killed."

"I'm not worrying," Jim answered, and wished clear down to his boots that the statement was true, for he was frightened.

"Can all the natives speak English?" Bob asked.

"You mean those with the professor?" Donald wanted to know.

"Yes."

"A few of them can."

"Good. Now, where is that plane? Howard said it had a cabin. How many women and children did they leave behind?"

"About fifteen or twenty," the Indian lad answered quietly.

"If we cannot bring them in one load, we can in two," said Jim, but he kept his fists in his pockets as they went to the shed into which the plane had been run. It took only a few minutes to get her engine warmed up, the Flying Buddies were in the cock-pit, and Jim turned to Donald.

"Is there likely to be more than one passage through the Black Woods?" he asked.

"There is only one. These men say they were climbing most of the way, if that is any help as to direction."

"Thanks. Don't give up the ship."

"Good luck."

No one waved when the huge airplane lifted off the ground, spiraled over the little group assembled near the water, with their dark-skinned guards standing close by. Bob looked over the side and saw a number of the naked men making their way into the wood to points from which they could give warning if the soldiers or workers connected with the settlement came to help the prisoners. From up in the air the situation looked even more serious than from on the ground, and the Buddies exchanged anxious glances.

"I'm banking on the fact that they were climbing up hill. As I remember it, we went pretty level for a while, then began to descend over a rough route," said Jim through the speaking tube, for the plane's equipment was not very modern.

"Hoping they'll come out on that hill?"

"That's the idea."

"Remember the chart readings?"

"Surely. I sketched the place and location for Captain Seaman," Austin replied.

"But suppose we do not find them, or find they have been killed?" Caldwell's lips were grim. "If we took that information back to the natives, the women would be slaughtered."

"I know," Jim nodded.

"Don't you think you'd better take word to the settlement? There are little towns around here and someone could get a note through to Captain Seaman—"

"And he'd get killed trying to bring them out! If we dropped a message, some of the natives might get hold of it, and Buddy, we haven't got a second to go down and find a white man."

After that they sat silent as the huge machine thundered up over the hills, past villages, white and native, over the ridge or the nearest range, over rushing rivers, and finally in the distance they were sure they saw the Black Woods which stretched for miles wild and desolate, particularly at this time of the year, when a funeral somberness seemed to hover over it and its ancient tragedies. On they sped, and at last Bob pointed toward a high bare clearing and there beyond the ravine arose the great stones of the ancient temple ruin, where they had left Mills. Eagerly the lads scanned the cleared place, then their eyes went over the ruin, but not a sign of a human being did they see in either place. Glancing at the dial clock, Jim spiraled in wide circles which included the two places, while Bob searched vainly for a sign of the professor and his kidnapped band.

"Maybe we guessed wrong," Jim said tensely.

"Let's drop down anyway," Bob proposed.

"Reckon I'd better," Austin agreed, but his heart was hammering against his ribs and his fingers were so cold he could hardly handle the stick. He shut off the engine, circled and finally they dropped near the opening Lang and his men had forced them to enter. For a moment they waited, then Jim released his safety belt, and prepared to hop out of the cock-pit.

"I'm coming along," Bob announced.

"Wish you'd stay here, Buddy. If I have to run for it with some of those people, we might be mighty glad to get off quickly."

"Well, all right." Bob slid into the pilot's seat. "I've got a hunch that Martin must be crazy. Wish you had some sort of gun."

"Second the motion, but I haven't. I'll pick up a club." Austin dropped to the ground, hurried to the edge of the woods, paused long enough to arm himself with a stout club, then leaped on the log and a moment later was hidden from his buddy's sight as he disappeared into the passage.

"Gosh all hemlock, I'd rather be going along with him than sitting here," Bob grumbled uneasily as he tried vainly to catch a glimpse of his step-brother. But, except for the swaying of the long vines which partially concealed the entrance, there was no sign that a living soul had entered the terrible passage. Through Caldwell's mind raced the memory of that awful trip with their arms bound and he felt as if he knew every inch of the route over logs, rocks, traps, streams, holes, snake dens—to Bloody Dam. He gasped, then he shook himself with grim determination. "Nice sort of codfish I've developed into—with a back like a jelly fish."

Caldwell proceeded to upbraid himself roundly for his lack of courage, but the recollection of those white women back there in the settlement, surrounded by grim natives who knew how to read the white man's clock, and were even now watching the minutes tick away made him shiver apprehensively. When the last one passed, if the boys had not returned with at least some of the women and children, alive and unharmed, the fate of Mrs. Manwell, her kindly husband, the Hardings, and any white men who appeared, was sealed.

"If we do not get there on time they will be sure we sent for the soldiers," he said softly, and he glanced at the control board, but with an effort managed to restrain himself from looking at the time piece.

He wondered dully what Jim was doing, how far he had gone, and whether he was safe or had fallen a victim to some section of the passage with its numberless pitfalls. Resolutely he searched the sky for a sign of another plane, but saw nothing, although once he thought he heard one. However, he attributed this to his over-wrought imagination. He considered starting the engine to keep it warm, then he remembered that the noise would drown any shouts or instructions Jim might try to call to him. Straining his ears, the boy tried to distinguish some sound, but only the noises of the desolate forest reached him. Not even the song or chirp of a bird relieved the oppressiveness of his surroundings. Cold fear clutched Bob's heart like great icy fingers, and his teeth chattered, as his brain called up the horror of the position he was in.

He thought again of the white women, waiting tight-lipped for their fate, whatever it might be; he thought of Professor Martin whose stubborness and determination to make the natives obey his orders had brought such difficulties, and this minute threatened the little band he had forced to follow him; then the British officer at the barracks whose wife was in gravest danger; and Jim alone there in the passage.

He shook himself vigorously, stretched his cramped legs, moved from side to side on his seat, and glanced about the spacious cabin which he prayed would soon be filled with the wives and children of the natives. He glanced across the clearing toward the ruin, and wondered what had happened to the Indians they had seen around the place. His eyes sought the tiny pool with its trickling stream moving so quietly one could hardly tell it was there, and wished he dared hop out and drink of its cool water. His throat and lips were dry.

From a distance Bob thought again that he heard a plane, but it was faint and he could not find it anywhere in the sky, although he searched hard, in an effort to get his mind off this anxiety. He knew there were several mail and passenger routes between the two countries but he was far off their course, so it was not likely to be one of them. There wasn't a cloud, even a tiny one, in the whole sky, so every pilot going from south to north, or back, could follow his course as easily as if it were a green line in a New York subway passage. He sighed wearily, and wondered what time it was, but forced himself to keep his eyes off the clock. He feared lest the limited time allotted had passed. Then, he sprang up, for far off he heard a muffled scream. It came from the forest and sounded as if someone were being tortured. Again it came louder than before, and with mechanical fingers that flew over the buckles, he freed himself from his safety belt, leaped out of the cock-pit, and ran as fast as his legs could carry him to the entrance of the passage.

CHAPTER XII
THE FIGHT IN THE PASSAGE

When Jim ran into the passage, he was hoping against hope that this was the way the stubborn professor was coming with his captured party, and that they were not so far from the entrance that it would be impossible to get any of them back in time to save the lives of the white men and women held prisoners. Glancing at his watch he noticed that the minutes had been ticking themselves away at an alarming speed. He took a moment to look at the ground and could easily see the foot prints made by the gang; his own and Bob's showed especially plain in the soft spots, but he dared linger only long enough to assure himself that none of them led out. Everyone went in, as he was going, which meant that, if Martin was in that secret route, he had not as yet reached the hill.

Running as fast as he dared with the light of his small flash his heart beat anxiously, lest after all, his hunch had been a bad one and he could not find any of the natives. He blamed himself roundly for not taking a chance to get a message to the barracks warning Captain Seaman of the danger in the village, and urging him to send a force with all speed to rescue the party of white people. Now, that it was almost too late, it seemed to the lad as if there were a dozen things he might have done, and that he had chosen the most foolhardy of them all; the one least likely to succeed. With his mind harping on this discouraging strain, his feet carried him swiftly on and on.

He thought of Bob waiting anxiously in the plane and was rather glad that his part of the task was not sitting still while the moments sped by. Keeping a sharp lookout on all sides, especially under his feet, he proceeded and made up his mind that he would not go very far. Surely the professor had sufficient time to be near the grade, and the boy calculated he must have come into the place by some branch route which the gang had missed as they were led by the reckless Red and his dim illumination.

Five minutes passed, then suddenly Austin's heart leaped hopefully, for he was positive that he heard muffled voices ahead of him. Believing that the professor was more than half mad because of his ineffectual efforts to push the work of the expedition and make better looking progress which would place him permanently in command of the work, besides bring him honors when it was finished, Jim restrained an impulse to shout to the party. Martin was sure to resent the appearance of anyone who might attempt to interfere with his plans, and also, he was well armed, the natives had declared. With these points in mind he proceeded much more cautiously, and at last he reached a bend where the tunnel widened considerably, then narrowed as it led over a stream. The spot was familiar to Jim and he recalled how difficult it had been for himself and his Buddy to manage with their arms tied.

But before he reached the bridge, he saw the secret way was well lighted ahead, then he heard a shrill scream and the rushing of feet, which seemed to be going away instead of coming toward him. Quickening his pace, he moved close to the wall, shoving along and screening himself with the hanging vines which were thick at this point. Again came the awful yell and the boy ran as hard as he could go.

A moment more and Jim was at the bridge, then he looked beyond to a lower plain and was astonished to see a man, crouched like an animal and running almost on all fours. His back was to the boy and from his lips came the piercing snarl which was enough to make anyone's blood run cold. Standing, as if he were paralyzed with fear, was the tall, thin professor, his clothes bedraggled, his mouth open and his eyes staring hypnotized by the awful creature facing him. Another cry, then the professor shrieked at the top of his lungs. Behind him were huddled the little band of natives, mostly women and children, while the two burly fellows brought to assist in the kidnaping, faced about and ran off as fast as their legs would carry them.

From a few of the children there came terrified whimpers, but most of the natives were quiet. The crouching man gave a shrill scream, mumbled something about his treasure, his riches, and then Martin seemed to come to life. He backed away, started to turn, but caught his foot on an exposed root which would have sent him headlong, but the man in front leaped like a monkey, caught him by the front of his shirt, and proceeded to shake him as if he were a rat. The powerful hands drew the cloth tight and tighter, until Martin's head dropped back, then Mills, for there was no mistaking the identity of the crazy fellow, raised him high above his head, and smashed him to the ground, where he lay still. Horrified, the lad stood, then suddenly he felt a hand on his arm and Bob was beside him.

"Can we get them out?" he whispered.

"I hope so," Jim replied.

Just then one of the native women saw the Flying Buddies, and Austin beckoned to her to come to him. She hesitated a moment, then, pushing her children ahead of her, she made her way around the murderer and his victim. Mills calmly seated himself on the dead body, searched through the clothing until he found tobacco, and rolled himself a cigarette which he puffed indifferently.

The one native woman reached the boy's side, then others cautiously followed, until finally they had all passed, and with thankful hearts, the Buddies hurried them as fast as they could walk up the incline, across the level stretch, and finally out into the afternoon sunshine on the top of the hill.

"Well, what's this?" It was Bradshaw who was awaiting them, and stared in wonder at the strange group.

"Help us get these people back to the settlement," Jim said breathlessly. "There isn't a moment to lose, Bradshaw. Gee, I'm glad you came along."

"Wanted to have a look at your friend Mills," Bradshaw told them as he proceeded to help. "Guess I missed the lad, for I didn't find him," he added.

It took only a few minutes to tumble the majority of the natives in the bigger cabin, and three into the helicopter. The engines were started, and the planes raced in a circle, hovered in the air to learn where they were going. Then Jim set the course, and putting on all the power he dared, raced the big machine as she had never been raced before, through the heavens toward the settlement.

They had gone a little over half way when the clock in the dial board announced that the time limit was up. Austin verified it with his own watch, and bit his lips anxiously. He did not give up hope, but prayed that Howard or Don, or perhaps the doctor would be able to persuade the natives to give them a few minutes grace. He glanced at Bob, whose lips were set, and his eyes scanned the route as far as he could see. Finally, three minutes later he made out the winding river and soon could see the settlement. To his joy he noted that the little group were standing almost as they had been left, near the boat, with Howard seated before his engine, and the white women and young people nearby, with their native guard.

As they zoomed at top speed, the white men turned their faces upward. The engines were shut off, the two machines glided gracefully to the ground, the native passengers shouting gleefully to the members of their families. Quickly the men who had been so determined on revenge, rushed forward and caught their loved ones in their arms. Presently Jim was out of the machine and he saw Donald standing near him, a watch in his hand.

"I find that you have half a minute to spare," he remarked.

"Yes?"

"Exactly. I held my watch, which is a new accurate time-piece, and while I did not object to dying when the three-quarters of an hour was up, I did object to such an unpleasant ending to the lives of my esteemed parents. It is possible, of course, that the hands stopped occasionally—barely possible," he grinned.

"Oh, I was blue when I saw how the time had passed," Jim said.

"Expect you were. Don't know that I should have cared to change places with you."

Then followed explanations from all concerned and unconcerned; Bradshaw learned why he had been urged to nearly tear the wings off his plane, and when the danger was past, the natives awkwardly tried to thank the Buddies by presenting them with gifts, while Mrs. Harding nearly went into hysterics, which the doctor hastened to bring her out of with a good shake.

"Buck up, buck up. Where's Martin?" he asked Bob.

"Mills met him in the passage and killed him."

The party looked sober.

"Twice you boys came through the Black Woods, but Martin, who forced himself under the butterflies, met destruction before the change of the moon," said Donald quietly.

"That's right," Jim nodded, "but it looks to me as if the curse of Bloody Dam was made so that fellows who aren't evil-doers may pass unharmed even through the Black Woods."

"Perhaps that is so," Donald answered, then went on with a smile, "And perhaps a kindness rendered a hunted lad named Yncicea and his uncle brought a blessing so great that against it the curse is not effective—"

"Perhaps," chuckled Bob, then added softly, "I don't mind telling you that we're mighty happy at having met that lad at my uncle's farm." Suddenly his mood changed. "When do we eat?"

"There is food in the basket," Mrs. Seaman answered, "You boys must be hollow as drums." She made a brave attempt to shake off the horror of the hour through which she had just lived, and Barbara Harding came to her aid.

"Let's brace up," she urged. "We'll all feel better when we have had something to eat."

"Suppose we take the food and eat it on board the boat on the way home," Mrs. Harding suggested. "I feel as if I cannot leave this place too quickly." Her face was white as if she had suffered a long illness, and her eyes rested upon her daughters, who were safe, but she dreaded remaining with them in the encampment where the white people were so greatly out-numbered by the natives.

This plan was accepted by all of them, so they made hasty preparations to depart, while the natives, the more reasonable ones, realizing that their act might bring serious difficulties to the tribes, pitched in to help, and many of them ran to their own quarters to bring presents as peace offerings.

"We feared our own women and children were in danger, or dead," one reminded Mrs. Seaman, who promptly held out her hand to them.

"I understand," she said kindly. "You need have no further fear from Professor Martin. He brought about his own punishment and I am happy that your families are safe." The man bowed low before her.

"We are your servants," he answered—but could say no more, for at the moment the air was filled with the thunder of many airplane motors racing nearer and nearer.

The eyes of the Flying Buddies turned instantly to the sky and were astonished to see twelve tiny specks in a perfect V formation, racing without deviating an inch from their formation, high in the blue heavens. Quickly the boy took out his handkerchief, broke a twig and tied the corners to make a flag.

"Fix yours the same way, Buddy," he said crisply. The planes were growing at an amazing speed into huge shapes as their pilots crowded on every ounce of power. The boys wondered how the captain could have learned of the trouble, for as far as they knew no one had informed the soldiers, but here they were and his heart sang with thankfulness that they would find peace and quiet instead of death and destruction.

"Here you are." Bob handed over his flag handkerchief, and Jim ran with the improvised pair of signals, to an open space, while the natives stared. He marveled at the formation of the thundering machines, one of which he saw was a bomber, and at least two equipped with machine guns. They were swooping now almost to the bend in the river, so Austin waggled a message to the pilots and hoped they would understand the scout code.

"All O.K.; All O.K.;" he waggled and instantly the leader's nose shot up, his hand went to the side of his cock-pit and his men followed him in a steep climb, after which they zoomed high, circled, while Jim went on talking to them with the flags. "Everybody is safe. No one hurt. All O.K." The machines made two turns above their heads, then the engine of the leader's plane was throttled and he glided like a great bird to the ground, made an admirable three-point landing and stopped. Instantly a man leaped out of the cock-pit and started forward.

"What's the matter?" he demanded.

"It's my husband, my husband," cried Mrs. Seaman and she ran to meet him. A moment he held her close, then braced his shoulders, and faced the others.

"A native sent a message that the village had been attacked and you were all going to be burned to death," he gasped.

"We might have been, but we are not," Dr. Manwell answered.

"Thank God you are safe, but, what was the idea?" the captain persisted. He had to shout because the planes were still racing near enough so that they too could swoop down if there was any sign of danger.

"Martin got a crazy idea that by kidnaping the natives' families he could force the men to push forward the work he was doing and enter sections of the forest which they feared."

"Great heavens, was he insane?" Seaman exploded.

"I should not be at all surprised," the doctor answered, then went on, "whatever ailed him, he has already paid the price of his folly. The natives thought that their wives and children had been killed or would never come out of the Black Woods, so they came back with other tribes, bent upon revenge. We can hardly blame them. They happened to find us all here; took possession of the weapons in camp, and before any of us realized the danger, they surrounded the women."

Seaman's lips were set in a tight line.

"I was busy attending to the pilot who has a bad infection, so did not know what was happening until I heard my wife scream. We were all surrounded, then Howard, who had our young American friends on a tour of inspection, appeared in the boat. Fortunately the lads had bombs in their pockets—"

"Bombs—"

"Yes and more in the boat," the doctor answered emphatically, as if it was quite usual for American boys to go about with explosives. "The natives were reasonable and the Buddies promised to bring the women and children back. They did, and all is well—"

"Thank heavens for that—"

"Let us all forget it, dear," Mrs. Seaman urged her husband. "The men were frantic with fear for their families, even as you were just a little while ago, and we cannot blame them for trying to retaliate. None of us was hurt, and now you find us quite safe."

"Surely," the captain agreed, then he saw Bradshaw. "How did you happen to be here?" he asked.

"I was looking for Mills, saw the expedition plane instead, and hung about to learn what was doing. After that, I did pilot duty and turned the helicopter into a passenger plane," the Canadian grinned cheerfully, then added, "I take it that further details of the exploit can be made later."

"All right. Now, Doctor, how about that pilot—should he be taken to a hospital?"

"I'll take him to my house and look after him a few days, if you have no objection. I do not believe that he is in danger, but it will be just as well if he has good care for the present."

"Suits me," answered Captain Seaman crisply, then he turned to his wife, "Care to hop home with me, dear?"

"I should like to," she smiled at him. "Before we start I wish that you would assure the natives that you will not punish any of them."

"Of course," he agreed. He called some of the leaders together, and when they were assembled, he shook hands with everyone. Speechmaking was out of the question because of the noise, and the tribesmen held up their hands as a sign that they were eternal friends. After that it was arranged that the doctor, his wife, Donald and the invalid pilot should be taken back to town in the community's huge plane with the Flying Buddies, or one of them, at the stick. Mrs. Seaman was to have a place in her husband's machine, Mrs. Harding and her daughters would fly with Bradshaw.

Presently all were ready except the captain, who paid a brief visit to the native's quarters, reassured them of his friendship and ate salt fish with them. When that ceremony was completed, they came with him to join his party. A bit later the planes were ready, the big one led off with its passengers and the sick man, Bradshaw followed, and last came the officer's ship. They rose swiftly, the British planes circled about them, received their orders by signal lights flashed in colors, and fell in behind the others, while the officer again took the lead; heading in a bee line for home.

Jim was as excited as if he were a part of some grand maneuver and tried hard to keep properly in the formation with his huge plane, which must have looked a bit odd racing among the other slim, efficient planes of the British Government. The boy glanced at his passengers, who seemed to have completely forgotten the dangers through which they had passed, and were thoroughly enjoying themselves and the trip.

Bob was, of course, beside his Buddy, and the two exchanged delighted glances. Austin wondered what his brother would say if it were not so noisy, but later, when they came down in the field's runway, the younger boy grinned widely.

"I've had as grand a time as a bob-tailed cat with a kettle of fish," he announced. "Wouldn't have missed it for a million."

"What I want to know is where you boys got those bombs," the captain said as he hurried up to the machine.

"If you find out, we'll pin a horseshoe on you," Bob promised with a laugh.

"Didn't you have a blooming thing?"

"Surely," Jim replied gravely. "My fists and an electric light flash."

"Come along in—I want the rest of the story," the officer chuckled.

"And, like the little boy by the cookie jar, you won't be happy until you get it," said Bob. Just then a pair of orderlies appeared with a stretcher, the pilot was carefully lifted out and taken off toward the doctor's home.

"I shall send congratulations to Mr. and Mrs. Austin on the splendid conduct of their sons—" Dr. Manwell began, but Jim cut him short.

"When Dad hears of Donald's trick with his watch, sir, he will keep the wires buzzing congratulating you and Mrs. Manwell. We were over four minutes late—" Jim said.

Bob laughed and changed the subject abruptly.

"I say, I'm as hungry as a flock of lions. When do we eat?" he demanded, and the party started quickly for the house and the larder, lest the young fellow devour them all then and there.

THE END

www.ingramcontent.com/pod-product-compliance
Lightning Source LLC
Chambersburg PA
CBHW061218210726
48294CB00006B/1888